P9-BUI-665

"Would you come with us, please?"

Two men brandishing assault rifles pointed them directly at Kyle and Rachel.

"She's not going anywhere with you," Kyle said. "You'll have to go through me first." He moved to position Rachel behind him, and they fired a round at his feet.

"We don't mind doing that," the man snickered, "but Rachel could save your life if she merely came with us."

Kyle glanced sideways, trying to take in Rachel's demeanor. Her jaw was set tight and her nostrils flared.

Her body was priming for a fight.

"Rachel, if you don't get into the van right now, Mr. Reid gets a bullet."

Kyle went for his gun but couldn't pull it in time. At first, he didn't hear the gunshot, but he felt the hot projectile slice through his flesh. Warm, thick fluids dripped down his side and he pressed his hand to the wound to stop the bleeding.

When he had a moment to gain focus back on the street, he saw Rachel stepping inside the van.

"Rachel, no!"

Jordyn Redwood is a pediatric ER nurse by day, suspense novelist by night. She pursued her dream of becoming an author by first penning her medical thrillers *Proof, Poison* and *Peril*. Jordyn hosts *Redwood's Medical Edge*, a blog helping authors write medically accurate fiction. Living near the Rocky Mountains with her husband, two beautiful daughters and one crazy dog provides inspiration for her books. She loves to get emails from her readers at jredwood1@gmail.com.

Books by Jordyn Redwood

Love Inspired Suspense

Fractured Memory
Taken Hostage
Fugitive Spy
Christmas Baby Rescue
Eliminating the Witness

Visit the Author Profile page at LoveInspired.com.

ONE

"Have you seen this woman?"

Rachel Bright stopped as the man shoved the piece of paper into her face. She stepped back and plucked it from his fingertips, viewing the photo on the flyer.

It was her.

At least, the person she once was. The scared shell of a woman who had been married to one of the most prolific, most feared—and most admired—serial killers of all time.

She covered her throat with her free hand to hide her racing heartbeat. Now, three years later, she didn't resemble the woman in the photo anymore, and the man searching didn't realize he was staring into the eyes of his quarry. Her hair was now dyed blond and worn longer, instead of the short, dark brown pixie cut it used to be. Dropping fifty pounds of weight had thinned her features. The only thing similar to the woman in the photo was the haunted look, which was now shielded by her mirrored sunglasses.

"Why are you trying to find her?" Rachel asked, handing the flyer back.

"You've seen her, then?" the man asked, placing the piece of paper back on his pile.

"No, but I work EMS in the area and would be interested in knowing if this woman is in danger." Rachel shifted her backpack higher on her shoulder and gripped the strap tighter to shield her shaking body from the stranger. Her years working in emergency medicine had made her an expert at hiding her feelings during a crisis in order to stay focused on the situation at hand.

And this was a looming catastrophe of monumental proportions. Some would say an existential threat.

"She's missing. Has been for three years," the man said.

"Who reported her missing?"

That question was like a hand smothering the man's mouth, silencing his words. No matter. Unbeknownst to him, Rachel knew what the truth was. No one had reported her missing. She'd been expertly hidden in the Witness Protection Program after her testimony had guaranteed her ex-husband served multiple life sentences for his crimes. The only people who ever looked for her were journalists scavenging for her side of the story or members of her ex-husband's cult following, who blamed her for putting a man they thought innocent in jail.

Or those who knew of his crimes and admired him for it. People were complicated.

The man chose not to respond to her question. Instead he asked again, "Have you seen her?"

"I haven't, but I'll let you know if I do." Rachel checked his shoulder as she brushed past him. Perhaps because of the pent-up anger over how her ex-husband, aka the Black Death, had forever altered the lives of so many women, including hers.

At least she was still alive.

"Let me give you my number," the man called after her.

Rachel did not turn around. At nearly every lamppost was her photo staring back at her. Still more people were handing out the photo to passersby. Rachel lifted the hood of her black windbreaker, further shielding her face. The wisdom of reporting to work when so many were seeking her made her steps cautious. How much longer would her changed appearance mystify those searching—no, hunting her down?

She reached for her cell phone, pulling up the contact number for Kyle Reid, the WITSEC inspector who had placed her in protective custody. It had been three years since they'd been in contact. He'd been the one anchor that had held her together during the trial. One of the few men, maybe the only man, she would call trustworthy. He'd held together her broken pieces while the world called for charges to be brought against her—assuming without evidence that she was complicit in her ex-husband's crimes. Calling Kyle would set her on a course of action she didn't feel ready for. A new identity. A new life and starting over again. She'd grown to love Springdale, Utah. It was the place where she found herself again—the true core of who she was—stripped down from all the accouterments of the two-physician-salary lifestyle she'd led before. Back then, she'd felt like she'd been living the American dream, until it all crumbled around her when, at their remote cabin, she'd found her then husband and the woman he'd imprisoned there for months. That was only the tip of the iceberg.

Shutting out the memories, she quickened her pace. There was one street that emptied into Zion National Park. The EMS substation was close to the base. Though the morning was cool, temperatures this summer were hitting record highs.

She put the phone back in her pocket. Her fingers tingled at her decision. Why were people looking for her now? As the result of being in witness protection, she'd intentionally stayed away from social media platforms. She kept one computer, for doing online research, but she tried to keep her digital footprint nonexistent, which meant not logging onto many of the popular sites for news. Breaking news rarely reached her until she got her newspaper the next day. Old-school but sufficient for her needs. One national publication was all she allowed herself.

Before she knew it, her feet had taken her to the base. Even though she'd refrained from developing close friendships with people, there was a camaraderie with her team that she enjoyed.

"Mornin', Rachel."

"Hey, Moose." The EMT had been so nicknamed for his bulky size. He readily owned it. Rachel didn't know what his legal name was, but he'd carried the nickname since his NFL linebacker years. His strength was useful when they had to carry people down off trails.

"How did nights fare?" Rachel asked as she approached her locker, opening the metal door and placing her backpack inside.

"Fairly qu—"

"Moose! You know we never utter that word. How many times do I have to tell you?"

He waved her complaint away. "If it's gonna be a bad day, nothin' I say is gonna keep it from coming. By the way, someone came here looking for you. Left you this." Moose reached out and handed her an envelope.

She opened it and read the words, printed in prim block letters.

I NEED TO TALK TO YOU TODAY. I'LL BE BACK AT THE END OF YOUR SHIFT. HEATHER.

Rachel shoved the note back into the envelope. Why had Heather, the only victim of Seth's found alive, come here? Maybe the Black Crew had followed her, which could explain why they were canvassing the area. Her reconstructed life was going to end. She was going to have to start over. Sadness enveloped her. A tightness at the base of her throat made it difficult to breathe. This was going to be her last day with the team of people she'd grown to love. People she thought of as family.

Moose's question startled her. "Did you see all those people in town? Looking for that woman?"

Rachel swallowed hard. "I did. Know anything about it? They say she's missing."

"Well, I don't know if *missing* would be the right word. Hiding is more like it."

"What do you mean?"

"Her ex murdered a lot of women. He's ranked as one of the top ten serial killers. Estimated to have killed nearly fifty women. She went into witness protection after she testified against him."

"You...followed the case?"

"Who didn't follow the case is a better question."

The station tones sounded, and a voice rang out in the room. "Gunshot wound. Base of Emerald Pools."

"Did I hear that right?" Moose said. "Gunshot wound?"

"Like I said...never use the *Q* word."

"Easier to grab our stuff and run there," Moose said as he straightened up from tying his hiking boots. "It's right across the way."

Rachel grabbed a trauma pack and followed him out the door. Moose yelled back for the other two techs to bring the rig.

On a sunny summer day, there were plenty of people on the trails trying to beat the heat. As soon as Rachel and Moose crossed the main road to get to the trailhead, a stream of people was coming at them. In the distance, they could hear the distinct sound of gunfire.

Moose grabbed Rachel's shoulder. "It's an active shooter. We need to wait for the police."

It was a standard in EMS—to wait to provide help until law enforcement deemed the scene safe. An injured or dead rescuer wasn't a help to anyone. Rachel couldn't abide by it at that moment. Knew she'd be in trouble once the chief heard about it, but she couldn't stand by and wait. No sense in worrying about being fired when she wouldn't be working there anymore.

"You wait here for them," Rachel instructed. "I'm going to go up and see if there are any victims."

"Rachel..."

More gunshots. "I'm not asking you to go with me."

"Yeah, but you know I'm also not going to let you leave me behind. Chief's gonna be mad if we die. He'll kill us again."

Moose behind her, Rachel jogged up the trail, stepping to the side as people raced down. Once people saw their medical attire, they pointed back on the trail, evidently signaling where the victim lay.

The trail narrowed. It was going to be difficult to do any work to save a life sandwiched between rock walls and thorny underbrush. That's when they saw her, alone, lain out like a child doing a snow angel. A plume of red on her chest. Rachel closed the distance quickly, her first instinct to place her hand against the woman's wound, a few inches under her left collarbone, to stem the bleeding.

"Ma'am, can you hear me?" Rachel called to her, reaching for her face and turning her toward her. Was she still breathing?

"Rachel…"

It was Heather…the last known of Seth's victims found alive at their cabin after weeks of imprisonment and torture. The other woman responsible for putting her husband behind bars.

Kyle Reid had just stepped out of his parked car when he heard the gunshots ring out. His stomach clenched. Hopefully, Rachel wasn't involved. He had to find her before something happened, and he was already nervous about the number of people he'd encountered who were looking for her. Hurrying from the parking lot, he ran through the stream of people charging against him to get away from the danger.

His standard-issue suit and tie with dress shoes did little for his agility on the sandy trail. Quickly, he shed his jacket and threw it off to the side, which exposed his firearm. Several people glanced his way, and it only made them run faster. He stepped in front of one woman and grabbed her by the shoulders.

"I'm a US marshal. Where is the shooter?"

The woman shivered underneath his palms. "I don't know, exactly. Not too far up the trail. There's a woman—she's injured…"

He dropped his hands, and she scurried away. Another few pops from the weapon forced his feet to move. The people running away had thinned out, making it easier for him to forge up the path.

As he took a hairpin turn, he saw a paramedic a few yards up the trail, and his breath caught in his chest. Even though she knelt in the dirt, her profile was the same. He'd looked at it for months during Seth Black's trial. Rachel. He was the one man assigned to her to keep her alive through her testimony, and then he'd had to…give her away. She turned, and he saw her face, easily identifying her button nose, high cheeks and soft lips. Yet, everything else about her seemed different. The way she carried herself. There was a confidence in her movements that she had not possessed before.

He closed the distance. Another shot rang out, hitting a rock formation close to him. Instinctively, he lunged toward Rachel, knocking her to the side, covering her body with his to shield her against additional gunfire.

What he hadn't expected was her coworker considering his actions nefarious instead of protective, and the stout man shoved him off Rachel as easily as if he were flicking an insect off his skin.

Kyle reached for his badge and flashed it in the big guy's direction. "US Marshal Kyle Reid. Back off and get your head down."

At his statement, he heard Rachel inhale sharply. She turned back to look at him, her light blue eyes wide.

Rachel scurried back to the supine woman. "Moose, I need you."

Kyle drew his weapon and tried to determine the direction the shots came from. He could hear sirens in the distance—local law enforcement coming in answer to likely dozens of 911 calls. He saw a metallic flash in the sun and aimed toward it, but he couldn't in good conscience shoot with so many tourists in the area. He shielded himself behind the nearest tree, which was like hiding behind a toothpick.

"Rachel, we need to get you out of here," Kyle said. He glanced back toward the victim. Rachel held a needle in her hand and was aiming it at the crook of the woman's elbow. The big guy, the one she'd called Moose, applied an oxygen mask to the woman's face and then dived back into their trauma pack. He pulled out a package of gauze and began piling the squares up against the wound, slapping tape down around the edges. The blood dripping to the ground mixed with the fine dirt, creating a crimson paste. There was a hint of iron in the air. One thing Kyle didn't like was blood, but Rachel's actions mesmerized him. She exuded tenacity. Something he'd not witnessed from her before.

No longer the mouse of a woman who could do little more than cower in the courtroom.

"Just tape it on three sides," Rachel said to Moose as he placed the dressing.

She inserted the IV and connected the bag of fluids. She looked back at Kyle. "Hold this."

Kyle glanced her way, eyebrows raised. "I'm the only one protecting you," he said, keeping the gun aimed at the tree line. "We need to move the three of you to a more protective place."

Rachel scanned the terrain, then looked at him, her eyebrows bunched. Her perplexed countenance was warranted. There was nothing around but high rock walls, small boulders that wouldn't hide even her slight frame, scrub brush and thin trees.

More gunshots. Moose grabbed his right shoulder, coming off his haunches onto his butt. Rachel placed her body over the injured woman while still holding the IV fluids up to keep them dripping in.

"Moose," she called out. "Are you still with me?"

He'd lain down more to keep a low profile than because of the injury. "Just winged me. Gonna take a lot more than a bullet to take me down."

Kyle laid a few rounds of suppressing fire up into the tree line, high enough not to injure anyone but hopefully low enough to get whoever was firing at them to seek cover. After he emptied his magazine, he wiped the sand and sweat from his brow and ducked down, pulling his spare from his holster and reloading. Once these bullets were gone, their best shot at a defense would be throwing sand. Kyle shielded his eyes, scanning the trees, his chest tightening at the predicament.

Then he found some hope—an indentation in the rock wall that would take them out of the direct line of sight.

"Let's pull her back into that cove."

Rachel glanced to see which direction he pointed. Moose gave a thumbs-up and crawled to the woman lying unconscious.

"On three, I'll shoot in their direction as you guys move her."

Moose nodded his understanding and tucked the small green oxygen bottle under his arm and grabbed one of the trauma packs. Rachel, looking far less certain about the plan, slung the other pack over her arm and put the IV bag between her teeth. Each grabbed an arm and readied themselves. Kyle inhaled deeply. He had twelve bullets left to keep them from getting hit. If they could get themselves tucked into an improved defensive position, hopefully additional officers would soon swarm up the trail and they'd be in a safer situation to evacuate the woman. Kyle lifted one finger, then two, then three.

"Move!"

Kyle stood, gun high, shoulders taut, scanning the ridgeline, sidestepping slowly toward the cove as he discharged his weapon. A flash in the distance. He fired two bullets in that direction.

He heard Moose huffing. Moving the victim off the sandy trailed proved harder than Kyle anticipated.

"We're going to have to lift her," Rachel said.

Kyle glanced sideways. They were trying to hoist her between them without losing any of their gear. He wanted to instruct them to leave it, but he also knew if the woman was as critically wounded as she appeared, they'd need it to keep her alive until the situation resolved.

Off trail, it was bumpier and more difficult for Rachel and Moose to find footing. Moose tripped, dropping to one knee, his hands raised above him to keep the woman steady.

Kyle fired another two rounds toward the tree line to keep Moose protected as he righted himself.

"Inspector Reid! Glad we found you."

The taunting voice came from the tree line. The shooter. Kyle's arms prickled. He continued to shuffle sideways to keep from falling. "Who am I speaking to?" Kyle yelled back. There was a mantra—if they were talking, they weren't firing. Male voice. Young. Twenty to thirty, he guessed. From his peripheral vision, he saw Rachel and Moose were close to the cove—not perfect cover, but in a better position.

"One down, one to go" was the only answer.

Kyle continued moving, listening. Silence was the answer. Had the shooter made his point and decided the battle was over for the day? Kyle made it to the crevice and folded himself against the rock. Even though the temperatures hadn't climbed to their highest point of the day, it felt twenty degrees cooler in the shade.

Moose and Rachel had the woman lain snug against the rock. Rachel was taking her blood pressure as Moose held up the IV bag.

Rachel lifted the stethoscope from her ears. To Moose, she said, "Blood pressure is on the low side of normal. The fluids will buy us some time, but we need to get her to St. George."

Kyle looked at the woman's face, and his blood

chilled. The dark hair, now with tendrils of gray, and aquamarine eyes were a dead giveaway. There had been two star witnesses in the trial of Seth Black, infamously known as the Black Death.

Rachel Black, now Rachel Bright, and Heather Flores. One alive and uninjured, caring for one flirting with death.

The marshals had scurried both into Witness Protection after the trial.

Now each had been discovered. How had that happened?

TWO

Rachel stood outside the trauma room at the local community ER where the medical team was working to stabilize Heather. Sweat trickled down the back of her neck despite the air-conditioning. Her fingers ached to rush in and help. It had been her job once, working as an emergency physician at a level-one trauma center, but after her ex-husband and his crimes were exposed, she'd left that life behind for safety. Her skills were probably rusty after three years, but doctors in these parts rarely dealt with gunshot wounds. In her old life, she'd dealt with them every shift.

Through the parted curtains into the room, she could see Heather's monitor. The bullet had collapsed her left lung, and the air and blood that filled the space were shifting her heart dangerously to the other side of her chest, making it difficult for the organ to beat properly. They'd successfully placed a chest tube, which was helping, but they were struggling to put a breathing tube in to help her oxygen levels climb. A medical team was flying from Salt Lake City to take her from St. George Regional Hospital via helicopter, but time was running out. Doctors called it the golden hour for a reason. Response time from Salt Lake was over two hours, and that was after they were airborne. All the closer air medical teams were busy. Rachel leaned against the wall and closed her eyes.

Lord, Heather has been through so many things. Surviving my ex-husband should have been the only trauma she'd have to deal with. Please help her overcome these injuries. Help the medical team make the best decisions and give them the skills and attention to detail to keep her from dying.

Though her eyes were closed, she felt a presence sidle up next to her. First, there was a sensation of heat caressing her skin. Some things about Kyle Reid had changed, but the one constant was his cologne, a mildly musky, woodsy concoction that tingled her nose. His presence in her city without a beckoning phone call from her end meant her worst fears had been realized.

Rachel opened her eyes and looked at him, reexamining the features she'd become so familiar with during the trial. Her hand ached slightly to reach up and touch his face. The sensation surprised her. Maybe it was needing to reconnect with something stable, something dependable from her past when everything seemed so uncertain again.

"Why are you here?" she asked.

Kyle offered her a cup of coffee. She took it from him and gripped it between her hands. His gray-blue eyes always looked troubled. Maybe it was the prominent brow line overshadowing them that increased the look of worry. Maybe it was the things he'd seen protecting the hunted that caused the look as well. His jaw was angular, with a hint of five o'clock shadow. Dark blond hair trimmed relatively short. Had she ever seen a smile cross his face? Had she ever seen a look of peace?

Not that she could remember.

A chill tickled her spine. Was it the words he was going to say or something else?

He leaned toward her. His voice was low. "How is Heather doing?"

Rachel sipped the coffee. Nutty and heavy with caramel flavoring. A hint of char. What else could you expect from a hospital coffee machine?

"We'll be fortunate if she makes it. They're awaiting helicopter transport to get her to the University of Utah Hospital. It's the closest level-one trauma center that had an available flight team, but between now and definitive care is a lot of minutes to survive."

Kyle nodded. "She'll make it. She survived Seth and all he put her through."

Rachel turned toward him, leaning her shoulder against the wall. "Bullets take down even the strong. Want to answer my question now?"

"Not really." Kyle took a sip of his drink.

"You've always answered my questions before."

"That's because I was getting you through the trial and ultimately moving you to a safer place. I'm not sure that I can say that now."

A nervous ache spread through Rachel's chest. The bitterness the coffee left on her tongue was inching through her psyche. There was no leaving her past behind, no matter how hard she tried.

Kyle cleared his throat. "They've released Seth from prison. He's a free man—for now."

Though Rachel was trained to take in shocking news and keep her emotions under wraps, this news tasked that skill. A man she'd divorced nearly five years ago upon finding out about his criminal behavior was now free to hunt her openly.

"How?" Her voice squeaked through her vocal cords.

"Juror misconduct. A woman with an extensive history of being a domestic violence survivor didn't disclose it on her jury questionnaire. Investigation has shown that she lied in other areas, too, during jury selection. Of course, they're going to try him again, but it's going to take time."

"He and the Black Crew are trying to eliminate any potential witnesses that could offer evidence against him."

Kyle puffed a breath out through parted lips. "There's enough circumstantial evidence to put him back behind bars, but eyewitness testimony persuades juries more. You were a very persuasive witness."

"Heather was more than me. Now she may not be able to testify again. It's going to be hard for her to survive this gunshot wound."

"How did Heather know where to find you? She's a long way away from Chula Vista, California."

It was a question Rachel was loath to answer because she had violated the stringent rules Kyle had lectured her on prior to entering WITSEC. Contact with anyone was highly discouraged, and he meant *anyone*, from her previous life. It was a quiet death. Something lived but not memorialized.

Her silence led him to his next conclusion. "The two of you were keeping in touch?"

Rachel felt like a child with her hand in the cookie jar. "We're the only two women that I know of who survived Seth Black. No one else can understand what we went through. I didn't think going to counseling and talking through all my issues with a stranger would be a good idea, either."

"We could have set you up with someone trustworthy," Kyle said.

"Heather was better. She's what I needed. How do I know the Black Crew didn't follow you here?" She pointed a finger at him. "They called *your* name from the tree line. You know they keep tabs on everyone. They've probably been tailing you since the trial. Time has no meaning for them. They're all playing the long game. And you came here, directly to me."

"If I hadn't, do you think you and Heather would have made it off that trail alive?" he countered.

Rachel bit her lip. He had a point. They could both be reasonably held at fault. Perhaps her first instinct had been the correct one—that the shooter had followed Heather here and naturally thought, *what else would she be doing here other than trying to find Rachel?* Particularly when news of Seth's release hit.

"When did this happen?" Rachel asked.

"They released Seth last night. Heather was informed. Did you change your phone and email again without telling me?"

"I had your number."

"If I had gotten hold of you last night, none of this would have happened today."

"So I'm responsible?"

He placed an assuring hand on her shoulder. "No,

ELIMINATING THE WITNESS

JORDYN REDWOOD

LOVE INSPIRED SUSPENSE
INSPIRATIONAL ROMANCE

If you purchased this book without a cover you should be aware
that this book is stolen property. It was reported as "unsold and
destroyed" to the publisher, and neither the author nor the
publisher has received any payment for this "stripped book."

LOVE INSPIRED® SUSPENSE
INSPIRATIONAL ROMANCE

Recycling programs
for this product may
not exist in your area.

ISBN-13: 978-1-335-58778-7

Eliminating the Witness

Copyright © 2023 by Jordyn Redwood

All rights reserved. No part of this book may be used or reproduced in
any manner whatsoever without written permission except in the case of
brief quotations embodied in critical articles and reviews.

This is a work of fiction. Names, characters, places and incidents are either the
product of the author's imagination or are used fictitiously. Any resemblance
to actual persons, living or dead, businesses, companies, events or locales is
entirely coincidental.

For questions and comments about the quality of this book, please contact us
at CustomerService@Harlequin.com.

Love Inspired
22 Adelaide St. West, 41st Floor
Toronto, Ontario M5H 4E3, Canada
www.LoveInspired.com

Printed in U.S.A.

And ye shall know the truth,
and the truth shall make you free.
—*John* 8:32

For Marcella Shadle. Thank you for speaking Truth into my life and for praying for me...always.

only the people choosing to commit crimes are responsible, but you can't stay here. We need to go back to your house and get some essentials, and we're hitting the road."

Would she even live that long?

Kyle followed Rachel's older-model red Toyota Camry to her home in Rockville, Utah, which was approximately six miles from Springdale. The Camry, covered with a fine layer of reddish-brown dust, was a far cry from the posh black Mercedes-Benz she'd driven before. Part of the suspicion surrounding Rachel was that she and her now ex-husband had kept many of their finances separate. This led people to believe Rachel had done so to protect her assets should Seth's crimes be discovered. Nowadays, that choice didn't seem highly unusual to Kyle, but the thought niggled in his mind, wondering if Rachel had truly had no inkling of her ex's other life.

One thing Kyle knew about witnesses—each carried a secret. Some harmless.

Some that proved deadly.

It was a hard position to be in. Many WITSEC inspectors couldn't see how Rachel could not be involved in or, at the very least, knowledgeable about Seth's endeavors. Many witnesses were duplicitous in crime. Long ago, Kyle decided it wasn't his place to judge their actions—only to protect them. It kept his mind homed in on the task at hand. For him, having that core conviction helped him believe that even bad people could be redeemable. His faith was a cornerstone to keeping that thought at the center of his actions.

All people were redeemable through hope and mercy.

That didn't mean his mind was always in agreement.

He exited his black SUV and followed her into the house. A completely nondescript one-story beige and brown home. It was shrouded in the shade of several cottonwood trees interspersed with a few ponderosa pines. He could understand why she'd picked it—the property would be hard to surveil from the street. Another departure from the home she'd had before, which had been a stunning three-thousand-square-foot Boston brownstone, which had sold for nearly $4 million. The only benefit to this property he could see was the stunning view of the surrounding bluffs.

Rachel unlocked the door, and he followed her inside. She locked the door behind him.

Stepping around him, she motioned him to follow and brought him to the kitchen. He sat at her two-chair farm table, which looked as if it had been rehabbed from a curb somewhere, and she grabbed two glasses, filling them with ice and lemonade. She brought one to him and took the open seat. He couldn't get over the change in her appearance, in the way she carried herself now. Before, her hair had been short, cut just below her ears. A double chin. Matronly dresses. She still wore her EMS garb, but he saw fitness gear strewn over the couch near a treadmill. Her hair was long, dyed blond. Only her blue eyes seemed to hold a vestige of her past self. She took her jacket off and draped it over the back of the chair, revealing a short-sleeve T-shirt and well-muscled arms.

"Am I ever coming back here?" she asked.

Kyle took a sip of the drink, letting the sour yet sugary liquid linger on his tongue. It was exactly what he needed to chase away the grit that lingered in his mouth.

"Would you want to? It's not exactly the living conditions you had before. You certainly could have afforded something nicer."

Rachel leaned back. "That would make me more noticeable, though, wouldn't it?"

Kyle chuckled. "You have a point. So, you followed one of my rules, at least." He twirled the glass between his hands, rubbing the condensation between his fingers before he captured her eyes with his. "You're so different."

She shrugged. "Many of the changes came out of necessity, to be honest. The first time I had to huff it up a trail to get to a patient, I knew I had to do something. It would have crushed me if someone had died because I didn't have the physical stamina to make it to them. I hid here for months and didn't venture out. I completely lacked cooking skills, so I learned to survive on protein bars and yogurt." She fingered her blond locks, twisting them around her index finger. "The hair was the most intentional change. Once the weight came off, I decided I really didn't want to look anything like my old self." She dropped her hand back to the table and grabbed her tumbler. "The physical change I went through is probably what saved Heather's life today."

He couldn't disagree with her. His legs still ached from the quick sprint up the sandy path.

"One suitcase for now," Kyle said. "We'll worry about the rest later."

She nodded and stood, resigned to her fate. He followed her, eager to keep her within view. They had to travel through the living room to get to the bedroom on the other side of the home, and the walls that he hadn't been able to see from the kitchen revealed something unfathomable.

Lining two walls were what Kyle would term murder boards. There were photos of many of Seth's victims, along with pictures of women he didn't recognize as known victims of the Black Death. He felt nauseated. His feet cemented to the ground.

"Rachel, what is this?"

She stopped and turned. "It's some of Seth's known victims. And some other women I think he might be responsible for killing."

"I *see* that." The images of Seth's victims were hard to erase from Kyle's mind. "But why are they all over your wall?"

Like trophies.

"I owe them," Rachel said simply.

"Owe them what?" Kyle asked.

"Everything."

Kyle placed his hands on his hips. Seeing this didn't support Rachel's assertion that she was unaware of her husband's misdeeds. It would lend credence to all the surrounding suspicions.

"These aren't good," Kyle said. "If people find out about this, they'll think you were involved in what Seth did. It looks like you have an unhealthy fascination with his crimes. I could regard these as trophies."

"If I study the victims we know about, I'll be able to find the ones they have not prosecuted him for. I owe them justice for not being aware of what Seth was doing for all those years. It's how I'm…paying penance,

I guess. I want the families of these missing women to have closure. Everyone is worthy of a grave. Something that marks the time they were on this earth. Families deserve a place they can connect with their loved ones when they're gone."

Kyle scratched his head. His hearted pounded, barely caged by his ribs. He couldn't wrap his head around her actions. Then he saw the scrapbooks on the table. He crossed the room and opened them up. Pages and pages of news stories about Seth's criminal run. Never had he seen a spouse memorialize the deviousness of an ex-partner in this way.

Unless they'd been involved.

He looked up. She was watching him. He swallowed past the tightness in his throat. The acidic lemonade added to his stomach roiling.

"Rachel, I've never asked you this. I always believed your prior statements, but I can't protect you unless I know the whole truth. *Did* you know about Seth's predilections before finding Heather Flores in that cabin?"

THREE

"I was never a part of Seth's crimes."

Rachel brushed past him, and he followed. She went into her garage and picked up a shovel. Going to the other side of the living room, she slid open the glass doors to her backyard and walked to the spot, a suitable distance from her home, where she had buried extra cash and new identity documents. If Kyle felt she was hiding something, this would not help. She found the tree, put her back up against it, took three steps—heel, toe, heel—and sank the metal blade of the shovel into the dirt.

Kyle had followed her out and was standing a short distance away with his arms crossed over his chest. "What are you doing?"

She threw soil off to the side until metal clanged against metal. She bent down and smoothed the earth away from the edges of the coffee can and wrestled it free from its grave. "Getting provisions."

Kyle closed the distance and took the rusted coffee can from her hands, flipping off the dirt-encrusted plastic cover. He reached in, pulling out several bound wads of $100 bills.

"You didn't need to do these things, Rachel." He put the bills back in the can and snapped the lid into place. "You had...*have* me. I know when I put you into WITSEC, I told you you'd be living a solitary life, but I thought I impressed upon you that I would always be here for you. Especially if someone was coming after you."

Rachel turned away from him and settled the shovel against the tree. He was right. Though she had planned and developed several exit strategies predicting that Seth and/or his followers would come after her some-day, the day it happened, Kyle had shown up as he had promised her he would.

Suddenly, there was a loud crash inside her house, like wood splitting from wood. Kyle dropped the canis-ter to the ground and unholstered his weapon, motion-ing her to step behind him.

She paced quickly to him, and they sidled toward the house, stopping near the sliding glass doors.

Before Kyle could peek, a voice bellowed from in-side, "Springdale Police! Show yourself with your hands up!"

Kyle secured his weapon and eased the sliding glass door open a smidge. He then raised his hands and slid it open the rest of the way with his foot.

"I'm US Marshal Kyle Reid," he said as he edged into the home.

Rachel followed with her hands raised similarly. There was one local law enforcement officer with a weapon drawn. Once he saw Kyle with his arms raised and Rachel following, doing the same, he lowered his weapon.

It didn't take long for the officer to notice Rachel's murder boards.

"Do you have a warrant?" Kyle asked him. When the officer shook his head, Kyle proceeded. "What cause do you have to come into this woman's home without a warrant?"

The officer turned slowly away from the photos and faced Rachel. "One, we need a statement from you regarding the shooting this morning. Two, we got a call from the hospital that the lady who was transported pleaded that we come protect you because your life was in danger. That people were coming to murder you."

"Fine," Kyle said. "You had exigent circumstances."

The officer was from the Springdale Police Department. Rachel didn't recognize him, even though it was a small department. She did, however, recognize the woman who emerged from her bedroom. Amanda Williams, a park ranger whom Rachel had worked with on multiple occasions. Since the shooting had happened in a national park, the Park Service would lead the investigation with conjunctive help from the Springdale Police Department. Amanda's hair was black, tucked into a tight bun. Her green eyes piercing.

"Rachel, why do you have these?" Amanda asked as she eyed the photos on the walls.

Kyle looked back at Rachel. She guessed this was the question that every law enforcement officer would naturally ask. Most presumed guilt before innocence these days.

"It's a project I'm working on," Rachel said.

Amanda came closer to her. "I can see you now where I was blind before." She reached up and fingered

Rachel's hair. The park ranger's demeanor changed—no longer the friendly camaraderie they once had. Just another thing Seth ruined in an instant. Amanda's eyes narrowed. Her breath was hot against Rachel's cheek as she spoke. "All those women—and it looks to me like you knew about it. What are these? Your trophies?"

Kyle stepped between her and the park ranger and faced the Springdale officer. "There's a lot you don't understand here."

"Regardless, we need to sort this out," the officer said. "It will be best to take your statement down at the station."

"She'll ride with me, and I'll follow you in," Kyle insisted.

The officer seemed perturbed but didn't verbalize his disagreement.

Amanda pushed Kyle aside. It surprised Rachel he'd allow her to do that. She was armed and clearly upset, the paint of anger red on her cheeks.

"I thought we were friends." Her voice broke.

An achy hollow opened in Rachel's chest. "We are."

"We *were*. How could you have kept something so important about your life from me? We've known each other for three years. I shared everything with you, and you kept this big secret from me."

Not anger. Betrayal. Rachel understood the disconnect in her friend's thoughts. Amanda had fled from a violently abusive man. Rachel had suffered far worse in her eyes. It was something they could have helped each other through.

Which was why she'd kept in contact with Heather.

"It's not her fault—" Kyle attempted.

Rachel cut him off. "I don't need you to fight my battles for me." She turned to Amanda. "I know it makes little sense to you what you're seeing here, but I'm trying to find justice for these women. There are certain rules I had to follow in WITSEC. I can't share why I'm a protected witness, even with those who are close friends of mine."

"Seems like someone let your secret out," Amanda said. "Otherwise, why would they be shooting at you?"

They sat in Kyle's SUV in the parking lot of the Springdale police station. Rachel's hands were clutched tightly in her lap, white from the force, and she stared out the passenger window. She had said little during the drive, sitting upright and pensive, and it was one of many times he wished he had a mind-reading device to get straight to the truth.

"Are you okay?" he asked.

She inhaled deeply and settled her back against the seat. "I'm worried...about Heather. About whether she'll make it."

Kyle wondered the same thing. He hadn't received any updates from Heather's WITSEC inspector, who was guarding her at the hospital, since Heather had gone into surgery.

"I need you to let me handle this police issue," Kyle said. "It will not be surprising if the Black Crew has been searching for ways to get you into trouble and get you confined to a jail cell. You're a simple hit if that happens. No doubt they know you're here by now. The media photos of you with Heather... You look different, but on close inspection—"

"I'm the same."

"No, you definitely don't look the same, but it's your eyes. There's only so much you can change about those—about the memories behind them. Let's get this done. Stay put a sec and let me make sure no one is waiting in the parking lot to surprise us."

Kyle exited the SUV. The sun was high in the sky, and temperatures were escalating. Reaching underneath his suit jacket, he placed his hand on his service weapon, scanning the parking lot as he rounded the front of the vehicle and opened the door for Rachel. Amanda and the Springdale officer seemed petulant, waiting for them at the doors. Rachel climbed out, and he placed his hand on the small of her back as they walked into the building.

"This way." The officer motioned and took them into a small interview room. Once inside, Kyle pulled a chair out for Rachel and then took the seat next to her.

"I think it might be best if I talk to the chief of police," Kyle said to the officer. "The longer Rachel and I stay here, the more dangerous it is for your community."

The officer huffed and exited. They knew who Rachel was and her importance in a national case. Kyle had taken away a big interview from a small-town officer, and feathers ruffled easily when that happened.

He'd retrieved his suit jacket from the trail and tried to brush off the debris, but it had little effect. There was fine dirt driven between the fibers of his suit that only a good dry cleaning could fix. It wasn't the image he wanted to portray—that of a tired, disheveled agent. He didn't want to give the impression that he wasn't good at this job.

Kyle thrummed his fingers against the tabletop and Rachel settled her hand over his to stop the movements. The warmth from her touch spread up his arm, hitting his heart like a jolt of adrenaline. He couldn't remember the last time a woman had caused this type of physical response. As soon as his fingers stilled, she settled her hands back in her lap.

The chief of police entered the interview room and held out his hand to Kyle, who stood and shook it. The more respect and humility he showed, perhaps the sooner he and Rachel could get out of town.

"I'm Chief Bailey," the man said, sitting. He stood about the same height as Kyle, putting him at about six feet. He was gangly—all bone and sinew with little muscle covering. His bushy, untrimmed mustache a compensation for his bald head. "You put a dangerous witness in my town, and you don't notify anyone about it?" he asked, his dark brown eyes boring into Kyle.

"Sir, it's not required that WITSEC notify local law enforcement of a protected witness in their jurisdiction. Doing so would defeat the purpose of our organization, which is to keep their new identities known to only a few trusted people. The more people that know, the more incidents like today are apt to happen. Rachel has lived and worked productively in your community for three years. Her talents as an EMS provider have undoubtedly saved countless lives. It's been a net positive for your city to have her."

From Kyle's peripheral vision, he saw Rachel's head turn, a look of surprise on her face. Perhaps she wasn't used to people paying her compliments—or maybe just men. Among Seth's many crimes was how emotionally abusive he'd been to Rachel. He reportedly never laid a hand on her, but his words of condemnation had been as damaging to her psyche as a punch was to the body.

"There's nothing you can share, officer to officer?" The man winked at Kyle, as if Rachel wasn't present. "Criminal background? Was she forced into hiding? Who is trying to kill her? We're in the middle of an attempted murder investigation. You've got to give me something."

Kyle pressed his lips together before speaking. "If you had spent even a few minutes on the Internet before coming into this room, it would answer the majority of your questions."

"Problem is, we've been getting reports that Rachel lured the victim here so she could be…executed."

"This information came from where?" Kyle asked.

"From an anonymous source."

Kyle smoothed his hand over the surface of the table. "Do you have any other evidence that would implicate Rachel?"

The chief tapped his knuckles. "Just her utter fascination with her husband's crimes, as reported to me by my officer."

"That's not proof of anything. I'm sure you could find hundreds of people across the US who are keeping tabs on Seth Black's case."

"None that were married to the perpetrator," the chief countered.

"Look," Kyle said, "unless you're making an arrest, we'll be leaving. Rachel won't agree to any questioning without a lawyer present. We came here as a courtesy, out of respect for your organization. Rachel will leave you a written statement of her account of the shooting, but after that, we'll be vacating the area."

The chief stood. "And dare I say, good riddance. We don't need her kind around here."

FOUR

Kyle took Rachel back to her home. The finality of packing and leaving her jewel in the desert was hitting Rachel harder than she'd expected. In this house—some would say a definite step down, more like a hovel compared to her previous lifestyle—she had found her true center. Discovered who she was without Seth Black's shadow stunting her growth. In the sand and sun of Utah, in the crevices of Zion carved out by centuries of clear, cool water running through it, she had been cleaved into something new.

Something strong enough to withstand the onslaught Seth was sending her way.

Kyle stood near her closet as she sat on the bed. A paralysis swept over her. Just like when evacuation orders were issued ahead of an impending natural disaster, they were under a time crunch. Kyle hadn't said definitively how much time he would give her, but she could tell from his mannerisms that the clock was ticking faster than the time she needed to catalogue her memories of this place. To sort through those things she needed to take and items she could emotionally leave behind.

He bent into her closet and tossed out several suitcases. "Rachel, which one?" It would be almost comical if the situation wasn't so serious. Like the comedies from early television, shown in black and white, the husband trying to get the wife to move, exasperation dripping from his face like the sweat streaming down Kyle's forehead.

"If you took your jacket off, you wouldn't be so hot," Rachel said.

"Why did you pick a house with no air-conditioning?"

"You said nondescript."

"Does ordinary have to be paired with misery? I didn't mean you had to be suffering. Witness protection isn't designed to be a prison for you."

"Isn't it, though?"

Kyle dropped the items he held in his hands and sat next to her on the bed. "It's not, but I get the sense it was for you. It's meant to be a new lease on life, but disconnecting from everything you knew and everyone you loved is hard."

"It's worse than Seth got. He still has easy access to his family, no matter how delusional they are in thinking he's innocent. He can call his mother directly. I have to use WITSEC as an intermediary. He has his horde of followers bowing to his every whim, even when it entices them to commit crimes. When people find out who I am, like Amanda today, they disown me and wish me convicted immediately despite my innocence. They're not interested in learning my story. I've been alone here, and even though I wasn't confined…"

"You feel Seth is living a better life than you, with

more freedom of association, even though he's behind bars."

"Not anymore. He's free and I'm running again when I did nothing wrong."

She flopped backward onto the bed. For so long, she'd put aside these feelings. It surprised her that she'd opened up so much to Kyle. Perhaps it was because he was the one adult she was supposed to trust, and with him she could be angry, be disappointed and let her true feelings show. She didn't have to guard her tirade for fear that saying the wrong thing would cause a backlash of poisonous words.

Maybe she had more freedom than she thought—with Kyle, at least.

Kyle stayed seated but took her hand in his. Rachel's heart fluttered. During Seth's trial, he'd been nothing but a tight, buttoned-up specialist. Not one hundred percent emotionally unavailable, but he exuded an air of professional distance. Any touch before had been only for protection.

This was not one of those situations.

Kyle had been true north for her during those dark days. She could trust his interpretation of the events that were taking place. He was loyal to her. Always timely. And though he never said a word to the media about her, the hundreds of times he pushed overzealous reporters and their recording equipment out of her way to and from the courthouse said more than anything he could say in words for print.

As much as she'd changed, there was a shift in Kyle as well. Little things she'd noticed from the moment he came back into her life. Bringing her coffee at the hospital. His curious introspection regarding her hobby of trying to solve crimes she knew Seth was responsible for. The first thing she expected him to do was order her to burn them—he hadn't.

More important was the way he defended her to the local chief of police. The kind words he'd said about her being a net positive for the community. She'd served years as an emergency physician and had never received such an accolade—let alone from Seth.

Something had happened to Kyle over the last three years.

He squeezed her hand. "I'm open to suggestions on where you want to go. Preferably someplace we can stay for several months until the prosecution is ready to retry Seth."

Her heart gently leaped. *We?* Did he intend to stay with her until the trial started? And through it again? Didn't he have a place already planned? Or was this just an effort to help her feel more in control of the situation?

"I have a place about four hours from here in South Jordan, Utah. A house that was willed to me after my grandmother died. I've gone there a few times to check on it and make sure it's ready, just in case I needed to leave quickly."

"Does Seth have any knowledge of the property?"

"He doesn't. I inherited it before I met him. It was something I didn't disclose. I'm not sure why I didn't. I was always very close to my grandmother, and I guess it was something I wanted to keep between the two of us—the memories that are there."

"Maybe something in you knew Seth was never worthy or didn't have it in him to hold precious those things that you did."

His comment echoed a pervasive thought in her mind. Had her subconscious known what Seth was all along and her conscious mind had stomped out the warning? Early in their relationship, everything had been fairy tale–like. The handsome young man from a wealthy family. They'd met in medical school. She'd gone through college on full-ride scholarships. Her parents, hard workers, were unable to assist with college expenses. She'd known all along that would be the case. When she and Seth were dating, Rachel had been enamored by the exquisite dinners, the fancy cars and the Boston town house he owned, where they would lounge and drink bottles of wine from foreign countries. Those accoutrements blinded her to some of the early warning signs. His anger toward her when she'd score higher than he did on exams. When he'd wanted her to pick a more lucrative specialty, like his neurosurgery.

"Ready to pack?" Kyle asked.

"No, but I will."

"One suitcase."

"I know. You already said that."

He released her hand and stood up, going back to the closet, and picked up the two suitcases he'd previously held. "Which one?"

"Kyle, I'm taking them with me."

"Who?"

"The women. The boards. They're coming, too."

Kyle had insisted they leave Springdale under the cover of night. They'd be harder to track and hopefully the Black Crew would take the night off. The four-hour drive to South Jordan had so far been uneventful.

"White Ford F-150 trailing. Looks to be a female driver," Rachel said, scrutinizing the car behind them in the passenger side-view mirror.

"Even in the dark you could make that out? I'm impressed, and I agree. I taught you well about peripheral awareness, and you've honed your skills. Is that person a threat, do you think?"

"Unknown. All depends on what she's carrying on the inside. She could overtake us, powerwise, but I think we're in the more agile vehicle, so we might be able to outmaneuver her."

That was always the issue. Those things that couldn't be seen. What was Rachel hiding?

Eventually, Rachel fell asleep. He understood why. Long days with scattered bursts of adrenaline always levied a heavy tax on energy levels. He was used to going without sleep during times like this. WITSEC did not afford to a normal lifestyle, and he'd never wanted to subject a wife and kids to the uncertainty of his work. Not only the time away, but the level of danger.

In moments like this, his mind would drift and he'd think about what most people considered a normal lifestyle. Weekends and holidays off. Dinner at home. Getting to keep track of an entire series on television. Seeing a movie in the theater. He'd had a lot of wild adventures. He didn't crave the adrenaline surge as he once had.

All that had changed a year ago, when a protected witness, a woman not unlike Rachel, had died in his arms. Shaking off the troubling memory, Kyle double-checked the address Rachel had given him and pulled up in front of the cottage. The sun had risen, and he got a good look at the property.

It was an upgrade from Rachel's desert abode. What would be the correct term for a high-end cottage? It wasn't a mansion, but more than the fifteen hundred square feet Rachel had lived in in Springdale. Two stories. A double staircase that wrapped skyward to a deck on the second level. Brick exterior on the first floor. Gray siding on the second level. Three dormer windows peeked from the top that likely had an amazing view of the Wasatch Mountains.

He looked at Rachel. She was slumped against the window. He nudged her shoulder, hating to interrupt the peaceful look on her face. She opened her eyes and stretched, accidentally hitting him in the face.

"Sorry," she said.

"I've suffered worse." Kyle laughed. The lightness in his spirit felt good. He felt a sense of peace around Rachel. He didn't have to pretend to be stronger than he was—not anymore.

He opened the car door and stretched. When he went to the back door to grab the poster boards, Rachel grabbed the other end at the same moment, and removing them became a tug-of-war between the two.

"Please," she said. "I'll worry about these."

He let the boards slip from his hands. It bothered him, her obsessiveness with these women, and he hadn't quite put a finger on if her interest was one hundred percent innocent.

He pulled their suitcases from the back of the SUV and followed her. She unlocked the front door and led them into the living room. It was kept up. Fashionably decorated in a French country style. Muted pastels. A lot of cozy furniture. A stone fireplace with an ornately carved mantel. Kyle set their suitcases down and walked farther in. The fireplace had bookcases on each side, which held photos. Kyle perused them, watching Rachel grow older in each successive frame. From the lanky kid to the heavyset, awkward middle school years that she'd grown out of during high school. Kyle's stomach turned at the photo of her med school graduation, with Seth sidled up next to her. From that moment on, her physical appearance deteriorated, the weight of Seth's abuse clear in the fact that she'd lost the ability to care for her own needs. Her energy had been focused solely to the care of her patients and surviving an abusive marriage. He lifted his fingers from the mantel. It wasn't dusty. Someone was getting paid to keep this place neat and orderly.

"Do you trust the person keeping tabs on this place?"

"She's been with me since even before I knew Seth. She's like a mother to me."

A person who was likely a poor substitute for the mother she'd been instructed not to keep in contact with anymore, for both of their safety.

Rachel stepped into the kitchen. "The only thing we'll need to do is get groceries. Nothing but cold water in the refrigerator."

Kyle followed her. There was a center island painted a light denim blue. The cabinets were whitewashed. Two modest chandeliers hung over the island, and chairs surrounded it. There was likely a formal dining room elsewhere. Kyle's phone pinged. He picked it up and read the message.

"Is there a television around here? Something that will get national news?"

Rachel motioned him back into the living area. There was an armoire off to the side. She opened the doors and pulled out the television. Turning it on, she then handed the remote to Kyle. He panned through several news stations before he found what he was looking for.

A familiar scene for him—an upscale Boston property with the periphery cordoned off with crime scene tape. He took the television off mute.

"Dr. Lewis was a fellow neurosurgeon in practice with the formerly convicted serial killer Seth Black. Today, questions surround his whereabouts, and anyone with information concerning his disappearance is asked to contact the Boston Police Department at once. It is feared that Dr. Lewis's life is in immediate danger—if, in fact, he's still alive. As has been reported, Dr. Lewis's wife came home to find a ransacked property, blood marring the walls and doors, and her husband missing. Since Seth Black's release from jail, several witnesses who testified at his trial have come under attack. One unidentified female is currently clinging to life at an undisclosed medical facility after an assassination attempt. Now this previous trial witness has disappeared under mysterious circumstances. Police say foul play is suspected. As of now, we don't know the safety of Seth's ex-wife, Rachel Black, or where she might be."

Rachel took the remote from his hand and turned the television off. "I'll be surprised if he's still alive. He was too easy for the Black Crew to find." She turned to him. "None of this will come back to Seth. You get that, right? He'll find a way to escape this just like he did the first time. Just like he did prison. And the only thing that will happen is more innocent people will die."

Kyle hoped she was wrong, but he feared the worst.

FIVE

Rachel gripped the handle of the shopping cart in the parking lot. They'd gone to a grocery store located two hours away from the cottage, hoping to prevent the Black Crew from nailing down their location. The news of Dr. Lewis troubled her more than she wanted Kyle to know. She wanted to present a tough exterior, but no one had firsthand experience of how brutal Seth Black could be—other than the women who had been close to him or nearly died at his hands. She carried those who fell victim in her heart always. Wanted to see justice done on their behalf. Now, none of that seemed possible. How long would she have to fight this menace? Would she ever feel wholly free of Seth—both mentally and psychologically?

What could Kyle do at this point? They could keep moving from location to location, but the Black Crew's fingers were like metastatic cancer. The unknown of when that one cell would populate another area and cause unchecked disease to grow was an unnerving, never-ending mind game.

Kyle walked a few steps in front of her, his head

swiveling from side to side, looking for any threat. It was in that same moment that a man rushed her, grabbed her from the side and pulled her tight against his body, the sharp edge of a knife pressed against the fabric of her collar. A slip upward of half an inch and her carotid artery could easily be severed. Rachel kicked the cart forward, reached up and grabbed his forearm, tucking her chin into the crevice of his elbow to protect her ability to breathe and shield easy access to her throat. The sound of the quickened pace of the cart's wheels over the pavement caused Kyle to turn around. Sensing danger, he already had his gun drawn.

Just as Kyle turned toward her, another man tackled him from behind, knocking Kyle's head into the trunk of a nearby car. Stunned, he slumped to his knees, holding the side of his head, blood dripping between his fingers.

Rachel, her heart in her throat, bent at her hips, pivoting her body behind her attacker. Once he was slightly off-kilter, she brought both of her hands behind his arms and shoved her head backward through his grip. As her head slipped through, he turned back on her. The knife flicked out with a glint of a silver flash against the sun, slicing down her arm, splitting open her flesh. Ignoring the pain, Rachel moved toward the cart and quickly grabbed a bag of groceries and swung it with all her strength into the side of his head.

Unfortunately, the bag of lettuce and fruit did little to stun him, and he smiled mischievously in her direction. Rachel reached behind her and grabbed two more bags. She threw the lighter one at his face to distract him and then clocked the side of his head with the second. The man staggered and fell to his knees, his back toward Rachel. She ran with all her might straight at him, lowering her body mass to slam into his backside, forcing his face into the pavement, and then wrenched his knife-wielding arm behind his back. He dropped it, and Rachel kicked it off to the side.

She looked back at Kyle. He sat on his haunches, his gun aimed at the other man.

"Can you hold him, Rachel?"

"I've got him."

Kyle pushed himself up against the car, leaning against it heavily, keeping his weapon fixed on the other man. "Put your hands up, turn around and get down on your knees."

The man ignored Kyle's request. Kyle pointed the weapon skyward and fired a warning round, pointing the gun back toward his assailant.

"I don't ask twice."

The man reluctantly acquiesced. Once down on his knees with his hands clasped behind his back, Kyle approached and cuffed the man's wrists with zip ties and then patted him down for weapons. He then got to his feet, holstered his weapon and walked to Rachel, swaying slightly as he got down to his knees and put the other man in zip ties.

After that, Rachel looked up. A few passersby had cell phones up, recording the whole incident. Kyle worked to get on his feet and approached them, gathering the handful of men and women like a father would wayward children, asking them with all the deference he could muster to secure the footage. Hopefully, appealing to their inner humanity would convince them not to put the video up on social media and put Rachel's life at further risk. Now Rachel wished they had gone to a store in the next state, closer to a metropolitan center, to throw the Black Crew off. They'd barely settled at their new location. Would they have to move again?

The yelp of police sirens drew her gaze to the road. Two police cars swerved into the lot. Kyle walked toward the car, where the first officer stepped out, his hands raised, and began a conversation.

The man lying prone on the ground rolled onto his side and looked up at her. "You think you're smarter than he is, but he'll get you. There's no way he's going back to jail."

Rachel looked down. The first thing she noticed was her blood dripping onto the pavement from the laceration on her arm, and she placed her other hand over it to control the bleeding.

"How did you find us?" Rachel asked.

"Like I told you. Just a matter of time before you have to face your fate. Flushed you out of your hidey-hole like the insect you are. Now all we have to do is stomp your life out of existence."

The words were not as eloquent as the man likely wanted them to be. Seth was highly intellectual and could persuade his followers with flowery words and speech. This thug's emulation of that had fallen flat.

"I've survived worse than you. I survived Seth once. I'm better now than I was then. And the only insect in this scenario is you—feeding on the death and destruction that Seth leaves behind."

Rachel zipped up her jacket and put her hoodie up.

* * *

Kyle shielded his eyes from the sun. Never had he been photosensitive. Now, even with a pair of sunglasses on, the light was too much. He was nauseated and weak. If Rachel hadn't been able to defend herself, the worst-case scenario would have happened to him…again.

"For the safety of my witness, I need to get her out of here and back to a secure location," he said to the officer. "We can submit written statements regarding the incident, but I think reviewing the security footage and…" Kyle reached into his pocket, gathering the contact info of the few who had taped the incident "…if you reach out to these fine people, they've agreed to share what they have as well."

"You're not worried about them leaking it to the press?" the officer asked.

"I may have said something about payment down the road if they kept it quiet. Not as much as they'd get from the press. Explaining it could put Rachel's life in danger seemed to seal the deal, if my ability to read people is still intact."

"That's quite a cut on your head. Sure you don't want me to call a rescue unit for you?"

Kyle looked Rachel's direction. "I've got easy access to a highly qualified doctor. I think I'll be okay in her hands."

The officer flipped open a notebook. "Why don't you give me your address and I'll send someone out for those statements?"

Kyle shook his head. "I'm sure that under the circumstances, you can understand why I can't tell you our location. There are just too many unknowns right now. I don't know who I can trust. Even if they wear a badge."

The officer withdrew a business card from his wallet and handed it over. "I get it. Must be a lonely place to live in."

Kyle took it and offered him a weary smile. "We'll be heading out."

Kyle waved for Rachel to come his way. He went to the car and sat in the passenger's seat, surrendering his keys. He didn't feel well, and there was no hiding it from her. His head was killing him. The nausea a close second in what would cause his demise.

Rachel secured her seat belt. He could see her sweat jacket was wet with blood, yet her first instincts were for him. "How are you feeling? You don't look well."

"Headache. Nausea."

"What's your full name?"

"Kyle Reid. I'm in some unknown city in Utah getting groceries. It's July."

"Can you tolerate a two-hour car ride? I've got meds back at the house that will help you feel better and supplies to stitch your cut up."

"I'll make it. Let's get going."

He glanced behind him and noticed the torn grocery bags piled in the back seat. The thin white plastic was splattered with blood. When Rachel was back on the highway, he watched their wake for anyone following.

"I've got you, Kyle. You taught me well. Please, just rest. I know to check to see if someone is following."

"I know you do. You already proved it to me."

He resituated himself and closed his eyes, gritting his teeth against the nausea. He'd never been in a vulnerable position like this before with a witness. Right now, he couldn't defend Rachel against a tick. Every time the car swayed, he wanted to vomit. He gripped the grab handle, trying to hold himself steady, and reviewed the incident in his mind. Mostly to keep his thoughts off how bad he felt.

Rachel was not the woman she was before. That much was clear. It was more than the physical changes and the few self-defense skills she'd picked up. She didn't need him. Maybe that was too strong a statement. She hadn't looked to him first, called out his name, when the man came at her. She'd just taken action. Had defended herself and subdued her foe without his help, even after being injured.

She was not a victim anymore. She was a survivor.

He reached out and touched her shoulder lightly. "Are you okay? Your arm?"

"I'm fine. Just rest."

His hand slumped off her body, and he pressed his face into the cool glass of the window. It helped a smidge. He'd never been attracted to a witness before. Always had held the professional line between his job and the client.

Now, that line was blurring. Her presence, her touch, caused a physical reaction within him.

Unaware of how much time had passed, he felt Rachel grip his thigh and jumped at her touch.

"Sorry," she said. "We're back."

He'd slept the whole length of the drive. As soon as he opened his eyes, a wave of pain and nausea washed over him.

"Can you walk?" Rachel asked.

He nodded and followed her inside. She directed him to the couch, but he stood in one place. He reached out to her, taking the zipper of her hoodie in his fingers, and slid it down. Her eyes met his, and she didn't resist his touch. It was almost as if she was as desperate for a connection as he was. He slid her jacket off her shoulder and looked at the laceration on her arm. It was open. Deep. Would definitely need stitches.

His mind traveled back a year to the woman he'd held, a witness he was supposed to defend, shot in the chest, who had taken her last breath in his arms. The witness had disclosed their location to her criminal boyfriend, who'd been stalking her. She'd been testifying to his laundering money for a drug cartel. She'd mistakenly thought he'd changed his ways and wanted to see him one more time. His goal in seeing her was to silence her testimony.

He'd been successful.

"I can do stitches if you tell me what to do," Kyle said.

She shook her head. "You're not feeling well enough to do that. Besides, we're taking care of you first. In a few hours, we'll see how you feel. We've got twelve hours to address my arm." Rachel reached for his hand and guided him to the couch. "You're going to let me take care of you by doing everything I tell you to do. I'm pulling rank as your doctor, so you must do what I ask." She put him through a brief neuro exam.

"Am I going to die?" he said, attempting levity.

"Hopefully not today. No focal signs of weakness, so I don't think you're bleeding in your brain." She pressed her hands against his chest and eased him back onto the couch. "Be right back."

He heard her go outside and start the car. She was hiding it. An extra effort to keep their location hidden. Maybe the garage was used more for storage than for a vehicle. When she returned, she searched the house and made all the same maneuvers he would. Checking that doors were locked. Windows shut and secured. She pulled the curtains closed.

Returning to his side, she had her medical kit. She unbuttoned his cuff and rolled up his sleeve. "I'm going to start an IV and give you some medications to help you feel better." The poke was nothing as brutal as he'd had in the past. Most doctors weren't good at bedside skills, as they rarely performed such tasks, but Rachel had been getting a lot of practice in the field over the last several years. She brought a standing lamp over and hung a bag of IV fluids on it. She took two medication vials and showed them to him.

"One for the nausea and one for the pain."

He'd never been so thankful for modern medicine. He could feel the medicine swirl up his vein.

"I'm going to stitch the cut on your head. This is just lidocaine—might sting a little. When was your last tetanus shot?"

His eyes closed, and her words became a sweet sound at the end of a distant tunnel.

SIX

Rachel stood at the window and opened a section of the vertical blinds. She'd paced the interior perimeter of the cottage, looking through each window more times than she could count, in the last few hours. For the moment, they seemed to have slipped through the grip of the Black Crew. Unfortunately, with so much heightened interest in Seth's case, she didn't know how long that would last.

Kyle stirred on the couch, and she felt it best to return his weapon to the table where she'd first picked it up. There were other guns in the house, but she hadn't wanted to stray far from his side while he was sleeping. A change in his breathing pattern could indicate swelling in the brain, but his respiratory rate had been easy and regular. Her farthest venture had been to the kitchen to get some dinner started. Hopefully, he'd feel better enough to eat.

He opened his light denim-blue eyes. They were clearer than before he fell asleep. She sat on the coffee table next to the couch. "How are you feeling?"

Inhaling, his eyes widened in surprise. "What is that amazing smell?"

"Spaghetti sauce. A secret family recipe."

"The Prego we got from the market, I take it. I'm surprised you didn't crack the jar when you slugged the man's head with it."

"It served more than one purpose. They likely won't use it as a marketing venture, though." Rachel chuckled and leaned forward, pressing the skin around his cut. "You seem better. A patient near death can't crack jokes."

He stretched. "Definitely better. The headache and nausea are gone." He lifted his hand in her direction, indicating his IV. "I think we can take this out, and it's time to take care of you."

"All right. But you need to tell me if you start feeling worse again."

"I will. I promise."

She took the catheter out of his arm, held pressure at the site with a cotton ball for a few minutes and put a Band-Aid over top. Kyle sat up.

"Probably best to do my stitches in the kitchen. There's better light in there, and I sterilized the instruments," Rachel said, picking up the trash and trekking that way. She stopped at the sink and pulled out the supplies. "I've already washed the cut out." First, she handed him a syringe. "This is lidocaine. Go into the wound and inject several areas, infiltrating the tissue with the medicine."

"Got to wash my hands first, right?"

Kyle turned his back and scrubbed his hands at the sink. It might be common sense, but he scrubbed his hands like a surgeon before going into the OR. "And these?" He picked up a pair of gloves.

"It's okay. Don't worry about the gloves. It's already going to be hard enough if you're not used to handling these items to get the stitches in place." Rachel rested her arm on the table. The cut ran from just below her deltoid muscle to the crook of her arm and was several inches.

After he injected the lidocaine, Kyle inspected the suturing material and then looked at the wound. "Have any dissolvable sutures? You probably need some on the inside to pull this thing together."

Though surprised, she simply handed him the requested item.

He opened the package and clamped the needle in the hemostat. With the blunt curve, he tapped her skin. "Can you feel that?"

She shook her head, and he pushed the needle internally through both sides of the laceration and approximated the wound's edges. A perfect horizontal mattress closure. Kyle had skills he hadn't been forthright in disclosing.

"You said you could do this if I walked you through it. Clearly, you don't need any instruction."

"As soon as I became a WITSEC inspector, my mother taught me a few things about sewing. She's an avid quilter."

"Why did she find it important to do that?" Rachel asked.

"Because she said no woman would ever want to be with me because I'd never be home, so I'd better learn some basic lifestyle skills to keep myself alive. I guess she considered sewing buttons and repairing torn clothing essential to life."

"I mean, if that button is the only thing holding your pants up…she could be right. Can't run from nefarious people with your trousers falling to your knees. You know more than that, though. You know the right suture material to use."

"Online videos are very instructional in a pinch."

Meaning he'd had to do this with another witness at some point, likely when they were on the run.

He clipped the loose string and then picked up the other suture material. "She gave me a motto that you're probably not going to like, though. She'd always say, 'It just has to be functional, not pretty.' I can't guarantee the cosmetic closure that you would likely do."

Rachel watched him work, numb to the sharpness of the needle. "Was she right?"

"About the motto? I guess you'll have to tell me after my job here is done."

"No, I meant her comment about women."

Kyle tied off and clipped a stitch. "It might be mutual, I guess."

"How?"

"Early in my career, I tried to hold down a few relationships. The unpredictable schedule didn't foster growth. Guarding other women became a point of jealousy for some of my partners."

"What about your dedication to your work? I have a feeling that didn't help, either. It's good for me, but…"

"No, you're right. After a few failed, short-lived relationships, I thought it best to just stop trying. Seemed pointless."

"You're not lonely?"

"Are you?" he asked, holding her eyes, and the question sank into her soul.

"Yes." Her reply was a whisper.

"Then why should my experience be any different from what I ask a witness to go through? At least I can still fully enjoy my family relationships. I can see my nieces and nephews at Christmas. I'm not entirely cut off. Having a shared experience, in some part, with what I ask my witnesses to do keeps me humble and puts me in their mind-set."

"So you can sympathize."

"Maybe *empathize* would be a better word," Kyle said. "I feel like the word *sympathy* means that I feel bad for you in your circumstances and maybe say some kind words about it, but I'm not going to do anything to help you. It's like watching the news and seeing a crime. *Empathy* to me denotes action. I'm in the dark hole with you, and I'm going to help you get out."

Rachel swallowed hard. She felt tears well up and turned her face away from Kyle. Maybe he knew she was crying and wanted to give her the space that he could while he did his work, which he was far more gifted at than he'd given himself credit for.

Her view of men had become skewed from being involved with Seth Black—living in his world had imprisoned her mind to believe that all men were the same when, clearly, they could be different.

In some ways, Rachel didn't feel she deserved another relationship. One, could she have a healthy one after the years with Seth? Two, didn't men always have an ulterior motive? With Seth, living a married life with a woman had provided cover. Surely a man with a wife and a stable, profitable career serving the community could not also be a serial killer. Looking back through her years with Seth, she had bought into this deception herself. Red flags she should have recognized she'd put aside for those very reasons.

But was Kyle different?

His touch was tender without being greedy. He wasn't expecting anything from her. He didn't dismiss her needs as trivial. Even allowing her to cry without telling her she was weak and needy was something she had not experienced with a man before. In medical school, she'd felt like she had to work twice as hard as her male counterparts for the same respect—particularly in her chosen field of emergency medicine, which was dominated by men. With her free hand, she wiped the tears from her cheeks. She looked back at him and offered a weary smile.

He gathered up the instruments. "I think I'm done unless you want me to redo part of it."

Rachel glanced down at the laceration. He'd closed it nicely, though not expertly. He'd done a far better job than she'd expected. "It's fine. Thank you," she said.

"Of course." He gathered up the pair of scissors and needle holder and placed them back in the pot of boiling water Rachel had used prior. "What type of dressing do you want?"

Rachel pointed to her medical kit. "The antibiotic ointment. There are a few nonstick pads you can place over the top of the cut and then wrap my arm with Kerlix."

Kyle followed her instructions, his movements sure and steady. He was more practiced in providing first aid than he'd let on.

"Did you try to date at all while you were in Springdale?" he asked as he dressed the wound.

"Is this a background question or personal interest?" Rachel asked. Another one of her bad habits—assuming nefarious intent behind any question that a man asked. Seth's interactions with her had often been piercing questions about her day and her whereabouts. She'd taken them at first to be a genuine interest in her wellbeing. Proof of his love and how committed he was. After a few years, her opinion changed. He'd asked the questions because he didn't trust her. Was obsessing over her movements. Stalking her. In reality, he was trying to determine if she'd discovered who he really was.

"Sorry," she said. "With Seth, there was no innocent question."

Kyle wrapped her arm snugly in the gauze and then looped the material to tie it in a knot. "Rachel, I understand why you don't trust men or wouldn't want to have a relationship. Why it would be easier to just stay single. Maybe we made the same choice for different reasons."

She pulled her arm away and settled it in her lap. "I never tried to be with anyone. It wasn't something I felt I could handle, or that I deserved."

"Do you still feel that way? After three years? That you don't deserve to be loved by someone?"

She couldn't lie to him and because she couldn't be

deceptive, she couldn't answer. Her silence was an answer in and of itself.

Kyle closed the lid to her first aid kit and snapped the locks. "What you've told yourself is not true, Rachel. You deserve to have a man love you properly. As an equal. As a partner. A man who wants nothing from you other than just to be with you. You've probably earned it more after what you've been through."

Her lips trembled, and she bit the inside of her cheek to keep from crying harder.

"It's been a long few days. Go take a hot bath or something. I'll have dinner ready to eat in an hour." He reached for her hands, and when she stood, he pulled her into a gentle hug. The stubble from his chin tickled the side of her cheek. His breath was warm in her ear as he whispered, "I've got you."

Kyle gathered up supplies to finish the spaghetti and rifled through the kitchen for a cutting board and knife.

He'd crossed a line with Rachel, and he knew it. Providing a comforting hug to a witness at a time of stress was one thing, but that wasn't the reason he'd embraced Rachel. He'd wanted to be physically close to her. To know what it felt like to hold her in his arms. It was everything he'd expected it to be. What he should do was enforce proper boundaries with her. For her safety. For his. Getting overly emotional with her would blind his thinking. It would put them both more at risk.

Above anything else, he didn't want to feel the pain of another lost witness. Maintaining a professional distance was the best way to ensure that didn't happen. No matter how difficult that might be.

As he chopped vegetables for a salad, he'd received a few texts giving him updates pertaining to the case. Heather was in critical but stable condition. He'd always found that phrase somewhat of an oxymoron but had learned that it meant the patient was still flirting with death, but their vital signs were stable for the moment. No news on the missing doctor. It looked like a kidnapping. No valuables had been taken, and his wallet, car keys and vehicle were still at the residence.

There'd been no ransom note.

Kyle didn't know what to make of it. Seth and his followers didn't seem shy about killing people in broad daylight. Why not just kill the doctor if they didn't want him to testify again? Was there really a reason to hide their motives at this point?

He set the table and checked his watch. He was about to holler out for Rachel when she came down the stairs, dressed in jeans and an airy light pink cashmere sweater, along with a silver necklace with teardrop earrings. Her long blond hair was down and blown dry in gentle waves. The citrus scent of body wash filtered through the room.

She wasn't making it easy to maintain any sort of distance.

"Feel better?" he asked, rubbing the back of his neck to dissipate the trickles of nervous sweat.

"Much. I didn't even get my dressing wet." She took a seat at the table. "You didn't have to go to all this trouble." She fingered the place setting and cloth napkins—the embroidery likely done by a distant relative. "But it's nice. I haven't had anything besides yogurt and protein bars in ages."

"Let me fix you a plate," Kyle said, accidentally dropping the tongs on the table. He grabbed them quickly and drove them into the mound of noodles, hoping the action would hide his shaky hands. Her physical presence was doing a number on him, and his rational mind was dissolving in her presence.

She could do this perfectly well on her own, but it was one way he could spoil her. Another action that blurred the distance he'd said he wanted to maintain. After piling spaghetti on her plate, he loaded it with meat sauce and sprinkled freshly grated Parmesan cheese over top. He filled a bowl with salad and put the dressing next to her. He'd found a bottle of white wine and chilled it quickly in the freezer. Now he poured her a small glass and then took the seat across from her.

The tension eased from her shoulders. A soft smile appeared on her lips. "You missed your calling as a server."

"In my household, whoever cooked dinner didn't have to do dishes."

"Aw, I see the fine print now. Well, I don't mind doing dishes." She took a bite of spaghetti, and a noodle landed against her chin, leaving a slice of red sauce, which she slurped into her mouth. She took the cloth napkin and wiped her chin. "I'm violating one of my mother's golden rules for first dates…or just eating with a man in general."

Kyle caught the redirection. It felt like a first date in every sense of the word. "What was that?"

"To never eat spaghetti for this very reason. Getting the sauce everywhere. It's not very dainty."

"No need to pretend to be someone else around me,

Rachel. You may look…delicate, but I know you're made of tough stuff."

"My mother was all about pretense. Not that doing your hair and makeup is an illusion, but almost putting yourself aside for the pleasure of someone else. I never felt like I knew to the core who my mother was. Only who she was in relation to my father."

Kyle sipped water in lieu of wine, though he wished he could have a taste of the sweet essence liven up his tongue. The last thing he needed was a bit of alcohol to lure him into doing something ill-advised. More than what he'd already done. "I've never asked you this before, but what was it like with Seth, in the early years?"

"If you had asked the woman who'd married him at the time, she would say it was a dream come true. If you ask me now, with twenty-twenty hindsight, I would say I was in a nightmare that I didn't wake up from until it was too late. What I took for love was a jealous obsession—and not over my being beautiful, but as a cover for his crimes. I was the facade he put forward so that he could commit his devious acts. It's strange. Even though I'm glad we're divorced, it still hurts at times, as if he died. Not the death of the man he was, but of who I imagined him…who I wanted him to be."

"I don't think that's atypical. Grief can be a normal expression of emotion when something we believe in wholeheartedly turns out to be not what we expected."

Rachel took a few bites of her dinner. "Some people would call me crazy over feeling emotional after divorcing a serial killer."

"You lost the man you thought he was. The life you

were building together. We all make mistakes. Some people just aren't honest about them."

She set her fork down and sipped her wine. "Have you?"

Heat spread through Kyle's chest. "Made a mistake?"

Nodding, Rachel leaned forward. "I mean a dreadful one. Something that you have difficulty living down."

"I lost a witness once." The words were out before his mind edited them. Clearly, revealing this secret could cause Rachel to doubt his ability to protect her. Maybe that was his goal. She'd proven she could be a partner. That she could defend herself. They would need one another to survive this. He hadn't ever been in a position before where so many unknown people were hunting his witness. In all his previous cases, the threats were known. He knew who to look out for. But the Black Crew was a completely unique element.

"What happened?" Rachel asked.

Kyle set his fork down and wiped his lips, taking a sip of water before he started.

"She was due to give testimony about a boyfriend who was laundering money for one of the Mexican drug cartels. Unfortunately, he also had a penchant for stalking, and it caught her up in that entire cycle of domestic violence. She loved him and had a hard time separating herself from him. Like you alluded to, sometimes people find it hard to tell the difference between obsessive traits and a healthy, mature relationship."

"I guess exhibit number one is sitting right here."

Kyle smoothed his palms over his thighs, trying to dry the sweat. His heart pounded behind his ribs. He hated thinking about that day. Why was he sharing this with Rachel? He'd never shared more than the bare details of what happened with his colleagues. Only what was necessary for the report and investigation into his actions. Reliving the day would open a well of emotion he didn't know if he could lock back down.

"What I didn't know was that she had disclosed her location to him. She wanted to meet with him one more time. Ultimately, I think she wanted to be back with him again and, though consciously she would say she was done with him, her subconscious needs overruled."

"I can't blame her. Some people can't stand the thought of being alone."

"When we left the hotel we were staying at to go to court, he ambushed us. He shot her in the chest. The bullet passed through her and nicked my left side." He pulled his shirt up and showed Rachel the scar. "The force of the bullet threw her into me. I caught her and laid her down. Fellow officers returned fire, and the threat was extinguished."

He exhaled slowly, picking up his unused knife, and tapped it mindlessly against the table. "When I looked at her eyes after that, I could see the look of betrayal she felt. Her lips, blue from lack of oxygen. I…tried…to save her. To do CPR. Nothing helped. They pronounced her dead at the scene."

The ache from his throat as he shared this tale spread through his body. He couldn't bring himself to look at Rachel. He heard a slight rustling as she stood from the table. He pushed his chair back, intending to stand up, too, but Rachel settled into his lap. Kyle embraced her. She placed her hands on his cheeks, easing her thumb over his lips. The other hand caressed the back of his head, sending electric tingles down his back.

"Rachel…"

She briefly pressed her index finger against his lips to quiet his protest and then lightly brushed her lips against his before pressing in. The wine he'd hoped to sip before now tasted sweet against his mouth. He pulled her tight into an embrace, his lips melding with hers.

She eased back, a soft sigh on her exhalation. "I just wanted to know what it felt like. To kiss someone who never intends to hurt me."

Kyle wanted those words to be true. Forcing a professional distance was going to do the very thing he dreaded. How could he keep her safe when his emotions were all tangled up with his physical attraction to her? He was flirting with dangerous territory.

He eyed Rachel intently, holding her gaze, caressing her arms gently and avoiding her injured side. "Rachel, there's always something a witness will hide from me. Always. I've never found an exception."

"I'm not hiding anything."

He wondered how long it would be before those words would prove untrue.

SEVEN

Rachel hadn't slept well. For most of the night she'd lain in bed staring into the darkness, questioning what she had done. Why had she kissed Kyle? She knew why—to prove to herself that men could be different. That a man could be attracted to her for who she was and not just what she could offer. That experiment had pulled hard at her heart. At the realization of how closed off she'd been to pursuing a close relationship with anyone.

It also proved to her it wasn't just a lab-based analysis. Something she could view from the outside and make an objective assessment of the study's goals. Clearly, she was attracted to Kyle. His kindness was tear provoking because of its uniqueness in her life. Because of that, the feelings she'd stifled over the last three years—of wanting to share her life with someone—were growing fresh shoots.

Throughout the night, she'd listened for him. He was sleeping on the couch on the first floor, putting himself as the only line of defense. After she'd kissed him, they'd finished dinner. He'd insisted on doing the dishes despite his previous statement. An attempt to stay busy, no doubt. After putting everything away, he'd asked her to show him the other weapons in the home and picked a small handgun for her to have in her bedroom. He'd checked the weapon to make sure it was in good working order—surprised when he learned that, every other month, she would visit this property and do maintenance. Making sure the guns were oiled and cleaned, so if she needed to fire one, they'd be ready. At varying times each hour, she'd hear him rise and walk through the house. He'd come upstairs and open her door, go to the window to be sure it was locked, and leave as quietly as he'd entered. Most often, she'd been awake, feigning sleep when he'd come through.

From downstairs she heard the doorbell ring. Rachel's heart skipped a beat. She heard footsteps cross the hardwood floor and then the sound of two male voices. She rose from the bed and put on her jeans and an olive green tank top. Even though this home had air-conditioning, it was still in the middle of the desertlike environment.

When she approached, Kyle and another man were in the kitchen, sitting at the table. The other man, dressed in a suit, was familiar to Kyle. Likely a superior in the way Kyle showed deference to him in his mannerisms. Kyle was scrolling through photos on an iPad.

"Rachel, this is Javier Armijo."

The man turned to her. He stood a few inches taller than Kyle. Olive skin. Jet-black hair. Nearly as dark, chocolate-brown eyes. His goatee was well trimmed. A pair of blue-tinged prescription shades complemented his black pinstripe suit. There was something about him that pulled at Rachel's memory. She'd met him before but couldn't put a finger on where.

Kyle's words brought her back to the present. "He's my WITSEC supervisor. There's been a development in your case that we need to talk about."

"You mean Seth's case," Rachel said.

He was short and to the point. "No. I mean a case that Seth's prosecutor, Elijah Nguyen, is developing against you…for murder."

Rachel's limbs felt heavy as she took a seat at the table. What she had hoped would never happen was now a probability. Seth had always told her he'd never let her be free. It seemed he was cashing in on his promise.

Everything about Kyle's demeanor had changed. It was almost as if they were meeting for the first time.

He positioned a photo on the tablet and showed it to her. "This is—"

"Penelope Schmidt."

"You know her?" Armijo asked.

"Not personally, but I've been looking into her being one of Seth's victims."

Armijo continued. "Twenty-eight-year-old female. She was a nurse at the hospital where both of you worked. Disappeared just prior to Seth's trial."

"Right," Rachel confirmed.

"Why did you think she was one of Seth's victims?" Kyle asked.

Why did you? Past tense. Meaning they had found her, and not alive?

"Seth had a type. Brown haired. Relatively fit. Pretty. He also had a radius—they found only one of his victims outside it. One hundred and twenty miles. Two hours' drive. The hospital dead center. It was enough time to be gone to hide a body, but not too long to draw anyone's suspicions."

"The cabin was that distance," Armijo said.

"Exactly."

Kyle rubbed his hands over his face. "They found Penelope's body three nights ago in the woods around the old cabin."

Rachel swallowed hard. She waited for the punch line.

"They estimate she's been dead a week."

She could see the multitude of calculations Kyle was making. That Seth was still in jail at that time, and she was free. She and Kyle weren't together then. He couldn't vouch for her innocence. A week ago, she'd taken a few days off and although she had traveled nowhere, there wasn't anyone who could confirm her whereabouts, either. A clear downside of choosing to live an isolated lifestyle. Was there someone who knew her work schedule and could have given that information to the Black Crew—in order to more perfectly frame her for the murder?

Risky moves like this weren't unknown to Seth. If she'd been working, it would have been an easy alibi. Regardless of what television purported, it could be difficult to nail down the actual time of death, considering the factors that played into the decomposition of a body. Time. Temperature. Animals and insects.

What had been done to the victim prior to death.

Kyle cleared his throat. "They found your DNA on the victim's body."

"What?"

"A hair sample. DNA matches your profile," Armijo added.

"Why would you test my DNA against it?"

"There was a tip that you were involved in the murder," Kyle said.

"Let me guess—an anonymous source."

To prove her innocence before, Rachel had allowed the police to collect her DNA. Fortunately, because of Seth's obsessive habits in erasing evidence from his crime scenes, there had been no trace of her at the cabin.

Seth and Rachel had married young. Each close to twenty-one at the time. Rachel had filed for divorce the day Heather had been found—almost ten years after their nuptials. She hadn't been to the cabin for more than five years prior to the separation once Seth stopped taking her there. It was a property that his parents had given to them as a wedding gift. At the beginning of their relationship, they had visited it frequently. Later, he'd gone alone, choosing it as a cover. Honestly, his solo trips had been a relief for Rachel. A break from his emotional abuse.

Kyle held her gaze. "Can you explain it?"

There was an edge of betrayal to his words. Seth had made it a pattern to always accuse her of things she was innocent of, acting like the hurt partner.

"No. I had nothing to do with her murder."

"Then how do you explain your DNA on her body?" Kyle pressed.

"I can't."

"So someone is framing you for her murder," Armijo said, a snide statement. He didn't believe in her innocence. Many didn't.

Kyle once had.

Now, the look in Kyle's eyes held an edge of uncertainty, and she could feel a canyon open between them. He was questioning himself. Her prior statements cast doubt in his mind, based on the way he averted his gaze. Likely he was revisiting how he felt about everything.

Including her.

"Yes, someone is framing me." Rachel searched Kyle's face. He wouldn't make eye contact with her. She reached for his hand, and he pulled it away. "Kyle, I didn't do this."

"Then how do you explain it if you've never left Springdale—your DNA being there? Your hair on the body?"

"I don't know…"

Truly, she didn't know, but she'd have to tell Kyle the truth.

Then who could guess how he would really feel?

Kyle's heart raced. His headache was back. Inwardly, he chastised himself. His instincts were correct. Clearly, she hadn't been one hundred percent honest. Many said the most accurate predictor of future actions was past behavior, and he'd let slide that Rachel had thumbed her nose at the rules and maintained contact with Heather.

In his disregard of the significance of that action, he'd let his guard down. Now he looked foolish. This coming as a surprise from a superior made it look like he didn't have a handle on his witness.

He stood from the table. His eyes bored into her. "You know how this might have happened and you need to tell me now." There were likely legal implications of forcing her to tell him. She could plead the Fifth. Ask for a lawyer. It intrigued him to know what she'd choose.

"I visited my sister in Boston," she confessed.

"When?" Kyle asked.

"Two Christmases ago. She'd had a baby. I couldn't take the thought of never seeing her."

"Any other adventures? Did you have contact with anyone else other than your sister and Heather?"

"No. That's it."

"Did anything unusual happen on your trip to Boston?" Kyle asked. Inspector Armijo seemed to melt into the background.

Rachel's hand went to her throat—her breath quickened. Panic? Difficulty breathing? Both? She pressed her mouth into her upper arm and turned away from him for a moment. Composing her thoughts? Or creating a believable lie.

She faced him. "Someone broke into her apartment when we went out driving to look at Christmas lights."

"What was taken?" Kyle asked.

Rachel blew her hair from her eyes. "Only items from my bedroom."

"Like?"

"My hairbrush. Toothbrush. The water glass that had been on the bedside table."

Now she understood the significance of those items. They all contained her DNA. How could she have been so blind? What she and her sister took as a teenage prank, a defense mechanism they'd both employed to shield themselves from feeling watched and hunted by the Black Crew, hadn't been just that. The Black Crew was collecting items that could be used as evidence against her.

"Did you report this to the police?"

"Of course not. First, it didn't seem that serious. We didn't want to draw attention to the fact that I was there."

Kyle pressed his fingers into the table. "You hid it from *me*."

"As if you would have given me permission to go."

"You're right. I would have talked you out of it for this very reason. Do you now realize how serious Seth and his crew are? They've likely been watching every member of your family since I placed you into WIT-SEC hoping for this very opportunity."

"I'm sorry," Rachel whispered.

"We have to consider other possibilities," Armijo said.

Kyle slumped back down into his seat. "I know."

"Like what?" Rachel asked.

"As big as Seth's network is, it would be difficult to monitor each of your family members for this length of time. The other option is they're getting inside information from someone in WITSEC," Kyle said.

"Like who?" Rachel asked.

"That's the million-dollar question," Armijo answered.

Kyle stood from the table and walked into the living room. He needed a break from her. He wanted to trust her, but doubt poisoned his ultimate belief in her innocence. The law and justice part of his psyche pushed him to consider that she was guilty.

His prevailing thought pushed those ruminations

away. Not that a doctor couldn't be a murderous leech. A woman, though? Using such violent means? That was unusual…rare.

If Rachel was innocent, then who in WITSEC would have as much intimate knowledge as he had? Someone who could predict that Rachel would break protocol?

The first name that popped into his mind was Dr. Nora Allen.

Unbeknownst to the public was the battery of hoops that witnesses had to jump through prior to being put into the program. It wasn't as if WITSEC just scooped them up and put them in new towns, washing their hands of those people and their lives. All went through a risk assessment with a Bureau of Prisons psychologist. The purpose was to help predict how the witness would do in the program. What would be their barriers to holding the line? The psychologist reached out to them every three to four months. Any information from the family to a witness or vice versa was supposed to come through WITSEC.

"How did you find out about your sister's pregnancy?"

"Dr. Allen called me. Gave me her due date. Said if I wanted to send any cards or gifts, she could help coordinate delivery."

"Did you do that?"

"No, once I knew the delivery date, I just made the plans to go back to Boston. I figured the fewer people who knew about it, the better. I could slide in and out—"

"Undetected," Kyle finished.

Armijo pulled Kyle off to the side. "You really want to go down that road and investigate a member of our own team?" he whispered harshly when they were out of Rachel's earshot. "You believe in her innocence that much?"

"I don't know what to believe, and it's not just about believing in Rachel's innocence—"

"Because you're probably the only one."

Kyle pressed his lips together. Hearing his superior's statement clarified Kyle's thoughts. Armijo didn't think he was being objective. That was a problem. WITSEC inspectors handled criminal types all the time. Justice wasn't always well balanced. Sometimes, it was about getting the guiltiest behind bars. Other people who deserved justice certainly went free.

"We're used to handling shady people," Kyle said. "It's the nature of our job. Whether or not Rachel is truly innocent doesn't change our objective here. Keep in mind, Heather's movements also seem known. It's not just one witness who has been exposed. Due to that, I think it would be in our best interest to do some internal investigation, because it would be nothing less than a firestorm if it came out before we investigated it ourselves that someone inside WITSEC was putting protected witnesses in harm's way."

Armijo considered Kyle's statement. "Dr. Allen also did Heather Flores's risk assessment. She was her contact as well."

In that moment, Kyle saw the red laser light land on Armijo's right shoulder, then heard a tinkling of glass, saw a spray of blood, and his superior dropped in front of him.

EIGHT

"Rachel, get down!"

Kyle barely had time to hit the floor before the spray of bullets punctured through the walls. From the direction of the projectiles, it seemed two shooters had descended upon the cottage. How could they have found them so quickly? One night and they'd already been discovered.

In his peripheral vision, he saw Rachel scurry up the stairs. At the first break in the gunfire, he grabbed Javier by the shoulders and pulled him into the kitchen. There was a large pantry there where he could secure him until they handled the situation. He opened the door and pulled him inside. He was alive, his breaths quick, a slight tinge of blue to his lips. Kyle pulled opened several drawers and found a stack of towels. He opened his superior's shirt and pressed the towel against his wound. Javier cried out in pain.

Kyle found his phone, but when he pulled it out, he noticed it had been shattered by a bullet. How close had he come to death?

In the rush of adrenaline, he hadn't even felt it.

He found Javier's phone and scanned the wounded man's face to unlock the phone, but he didn't find a good signal. No bars, but he still tried to call 911. The call didn't go through. He sent a text message to their headquarters and prayed it would find home. Though headquarters was miles away in another state, hopefully they could notify local law enforcement and a rescue unit.

"Javier, you need to hold pressure to the wound. I've got to get out of here to help Rachel before they pin me down." He pulled Armijo's weapon from his holster and put it on his belly. "If you hear someone coming, shoot unless they announce themselves." Javier nodded, his face glistening with sweat, reflective of both pain and fear. Though they handled dangerous witnesses often, it wasn't every day they took oncoming fire.

Kyle exited the pantry and looked at the floor. There was a definitive blood trail that led from where Javier had fallen to his current position in the pantry like grisly breadcrumbs. Nothing Kyle could do about it now. Since the first barrage of gunfire, Kyle hadn't heard anything, and all the doors remained closed.

With his weapon at his side, he paced back to the living room and peeked out the window. He didn't see anyone. Where had they gone? What was their plan? To kill Rachel or take her with them? He was hurrying toward the back of the house, toward the screened-in porch, when he heard the explosion toward the front of the house.

He had to give them credit for the awe factor. They weren't attempting to be stealthy in any measure.

Kyle exited the screened-in porch to the backyard

and made his way to the front of the house. He moved quickly, knowing that as soon as the gunmen found the red trail leading them straight to Javier's position, Armijo would have little time or strength to defend himself. When he rounded to the front of the house, he saw smoke clawing its way toward the peaceful blue sky. A small, likely improvised, explosive device had obliterated the entryway. He stepped through the hole, acrid smoke filling his nostrils. Part of the wood frame was on fire. If that wasn't controlled, it could take the whole house, but his priorities were making sure Javier and Rachel got out alive.

Making his way through the rubble, his gun held out ahead of him, his eyes roving to keep any potential targets in his sight, he found the first gunman heading into the kitchen carrying a weapon that was more powerful than needed for the intended job. As the man reared the weapon up to shoot through the closed pantry door, Kyle laid a round into his back, and the man dropped. Kyle approached him quickly, taking the automatic assault rifle from his hands and holstering his own weapon. Likely, his partner was using the same armament.

Kyle bent down to one knee. The man's face was toward him, his eyes open, but it was clear he could not move his arms or legs. He was breathing, but his shoulders heaved with each attempt. The shot had landed in the man's back, exactly midline. If he had to make his own medical diagnosis, the shot had pierced his spinal cord. He was no longer a threat, and the difficulty breathing would make it impossible for him to yell out and warn his partner.

Now to find Rachel.

* * *

Rachel bounded up the steps and went into the main bedroom. In there, she had several weapons hidden for an occasion such as this. From her nightstand, she pulled out her handgun. From the same drawer, she pulled out a sheath that held a large knife. Quickly, she lifted her pant leg and secured the knife. If things got close, that knife would be her last line of defense.

In less than three days, she'd been hunted three times. Instead of making her wearier, it made her angry. *Why do I have to spend my life running when I didn't do anything wrong? Getting mixed up with the wrong man shouldn't be a life sentence.*

A resolve set within her. She'd been hiding for three years like she was the guilty one, holding a defensive position and praying that this day would never happen. It wasn't that she'd become the next ninja warrior, but she had taken it upon herself to learn a few things for just this scenario.

Because if she knew anything about Seth, she knew he'd never give up on trying to kill her unless he was dead himself.

Well, I'm not running anymore.

Rachel stepped out of the bedroom. She had a plan. She didn't know if it was a wise one, but if it worked, she could dispense with the situation quickly.

She'd seen Inspector Armijo go down and hadn't waited to see any additional fallout. Kyle was armed and better trained. Hopefully, he was still engaged in the situation, because there seemed to be more than one person trying to eliminate them.

She peeked out into the hallway. The only sound

was that of a door closing on the first floor. Someone was moving around below. Hopefully Kyle. She patted her back pocket and then remembered her phone sat on the kitchen table downstairs. No calling for help in the short term.

If Kyle was down or otherwise detained, she was on her own. Just like she had been for years.

The sound of the explosion pushed her back into the bedroom. The smell of smoke wafted up to the second floor. She had to give Seth credit. Why had he changed his MO so much? These attacks had been in daylight. Full-frontal assault. It would be easy to identify the assailants.

Which meant they hadn't figured they would leave anyone alive to make an ID.

Rachel pressed her back against the wall next to the open door. Just because she was going on the offensive didn't mean her body didn't feel every ounce of her fear. Her fingertips tingled. She forced herself to take slower, deeper breaths. If she continued to hyperventilate, her hands would cramp and she'd be unable to hold a weapon.

Stepping out onto the landing, she looked down the stairs and made eye contact with a black-clad assailant with a ski mask over his face. He reared his weapon toward her and fired off a multitude of successive shots.

Rachel scurried back into the bedroom. The doors to the closet at the end of the hallway shattered. Broken remnants of splintered wood and drywall showered her face.

Part one of her plan was complete. The assailant knew where she was and would come after her.

She skirted to the other side of the bedroom and went into the bathroom, closing the door and locking it, and then paced through it to the bedroom on the other side.

Veiled from her attacker, she hid behind the door and waited for the black blur to run past the doorway. After he did, Rachel darted into the hall, tracing his steps, and found him at the bathroom door, poising the weapon to fire at the lock.

"Drop your weapon or I'll shoot you," she stated to the figure from the doorway. His shoulders eased down as he contemplated his next move.

The masked assailant dropped his left shoulder, not in a motion to surrender, but in a move to flip his direction and fire at her. Rachel released a round before he could fully turn, hitting his body on the left lower side. He tumbled to the floor, clutching his back.

That's when she felt someone rush up behind her. She almost turned and fired when Kyle wrapped his arms around her waist, bringing his hand up to her arm and drawing down her weapon.

"Great job, Rachel. I've got this guy. Armijo is in the pantry. He needs your help."

Rachel pocketed her gun and headed down the stairs. The front entryway was fully engulfed in flames. She stifled a cough as she rounded into the kitchen.

First, Rachel came upon the body of the first assailant. A gunshot wound to the back. Kyle had restrained his hands. The ski mask was askew, and Rachel took it off his head. The man's eyes were closed. He was still breathing, but too slowly. Rachel figured he wasn't long for this world.

Grabbing the man by the legs, she pulled him back

and opened the pantry door...and came face-to-face with Javier Armijo raising a weapon with shaky hands, his finger settling on the trigger.

She instinctively lifted her hands in surrender. "It's Rachel!"

Armijo dropped the weapon to the side, and Rachel stepped in and knelt down next to him.

"Can I see?" she asked, taking one of his trembling hands in hers.

He nodded assent. She pulled open his shirt, exposing the wound to his upper right shoulder. Considering his difficulty breathing, he'd likely collapsed his lung. She backed out of the space and headed into the kitchen to get her medical kit. Stepping next to the sink, she grabbed a pitcher and set it in the sink to fill it with water. From the trash, she gathered the IV tubing she'd used on Kyle. Not sanitary, but she had little choice in the moment.

Honestly, she didn't know if the maneuver was going to work. But she had no alternative. They were miles away from the nearest trauma center, and local EMS were likely first responders and probably didn't carry any advanced medical equipment.

Kyle came up behind her. "We need to move Javier onto the dining room table," Rachel said.

As she turned, a beam from over the front doorway fell to the floor, burning embers cascading down like fireworks. The beloved cottage, the last remnant of her life that she could fully claim as her own, was falling around her. All that her grandmother had left for her, torched by Seth's darkness. Losing this piece of serenity was making Rachel feel unhinged. Even if she beat

Seth in this current chess match, there was nothing left for her to go back to. She shut the thoughts down and forced herself to focus on her patient. They entered the pantry, and Rachel pulled Javier by the ankles as Kyle leaned over and scooped him up by the shoulders.

They wrestled him onto the table. Rachel pulled all the chairs from one side away so she'd have easy access to perform the procedure. Kyle raced back to the pantry to gather additional supplies, and Rachel grabbed a few needed items from the kitchen.

Standing next to Javier, as his color paled and his skin dotted with droplets of sweat, she opened a clean kitchen towel and placed the instruments she'd use on top. This didn't match the sterile procedure in the hospital, but habit forced her to at least try to do all she could for her patient under these circumstances. Secondary infection could be just as brutal a killer as the primary injury.

"Help me get his jacket and shirt off," Rachel ordered. Each took a shoulder and lifted, wrestling him out of his clothes. Rachel cupped his head as they laid him back down on the table. Javier was not responsive other than a few moans as they moved him.

Rachel yanked several disinfectant hand wipes from a canister. Iodine was the preferred antiseptic, but this would have to do. She scrubbed his side and then picked up a scalpel, palpating down his rib cage to the spot between the ribs she'd need to cut into. "This is going to hurt." She sliced through his skin. Javier reared up slightly and protested. Not a strong yell, which would have been reassuring, but a huffed-out mew because of his body's lack of oxygen and his inability to take a deep breath. Her patient continued to try to sit up. Swatted at her hands to drive them away.

Kyle gripped his shoulders and forced him back down to the table. "It's okay. She's helping you."

Armijo blinked rapidly. "You…sure?"

Rachel knew Javier didn't believe in her innocence, and she also knew he'd likely chastised Kyle for giving any credence to her assertion that she had nothing to do with Penelope Schmidt's murder.

Sweat poured from Armijo's face. Kyle grabbed an extra towel from the pile and wiped it clear. "I'm sure," he said, attempting to reassure his coworker.

"Sorry, a little more pain." She pushed her index finger between the ribs, the IV tubing nestled next to it, through the incision, and left the tubing behind. Taking the pitcher of water, she pulled a chair back next to her and settled the end in the water. A poor man's chest tube with tubing that had too small a lumen, but despite the hindrances, air and blood bubbled through the water. Not as fast of a pace as she hoped, but the measure should buy him some time.

Rachel returned her attention to her patient and stitched tight the skin around the IV tubing. From her kit, she grabbed some gauze and smothered it with antibiotic ointment, placing it around the site and securing it in place with foam tape.

"Can you go find him a blanket?" Rachel asked Kyle.

"Of course."

Kyle skirted off. Rachel laid a reassuring hand on her patient. No matter his attitude or opinion about her, she was a physician at heart and had a duty to treat.

Could she blame him for his feelings? He wasn't in the minority.

"Thank…you," he said. "My…breathing…little easier." She patted his hand, but he gripped hers in response. When patients felt near to death, they always reached out. At that moment, thoughts, feelings, barriers didn't matter. Just a human touch. Not wanting to be alone.

And yet that's the sentence she'd been living out. Being alone. Forced to, in some senses. Voluntarily in others.

"I've bought you some time, but we need to get you to a hospital quickly," she reassured him.

Finally, the welcoming sound of sirens came from the distance. At the right time. The smoke from the front entryway was starting to billow more into the house.

"I may have been…wrong about…you."

Rachel was relieved both by his words and his ability to string more words together, even though his speech was still choppy. It meant the tube was helping with his breathing.

Kyle returned and laid the blanket on Javier. "You look better. A bit of color."

"How's the man upstairs?" Rachel asked.

"He'll live. He's breathing fine. I shredded a few bed linens to put a dressing in place to control the bleeding. More than he deserves. How about the other guy down here?"

"Depends on the capability of the responding EMS. He needs help breathing and oxygen pretty quickly if he's going to survive."

The acrid smoke caused Kyle to cough. "We need to

start moving people out of here. It won't take long for that entry fire to take hold."

In that moment, there were men at the back door, in EMS uniforms, carrying a backboard. They could use that to get Javier to safety. He'd be her choice to evacuate first.

It tore Rachel's soul seeing the gunman lying there in distress. Emergency medicine was all about triage. It wasn't a fair system but a necessary one. Using the available resources to help those that could be saved. The bullet wound to the back. The lack of movement to the extremities. How the man's shoulders heaved to take each breath showed a high spinal cord injury. She could have used her knowledge and slim medical supplies to save him, but she'd chosen Javier instead.

Kyle waved the EMTs over. At the same moment, water spray spewed into the home. A team of firefighters was working to knock down the flames at the front door.

Rachel held a hand up. "Turn him toward me and put the board underneath." They did as she instructed and moved him onto the hard blue plastic. Rachel grabbed the pitcher of water. "You need to keep this next to him or lower to help get the air out of his chest."

"We got it. We'll get him to the rig and start a line and oxygen."

When this story came to light, they would judge Rachel for picking Inspector Armijo over the more injured assailant, and few would be interested in her explanation of the principles of triage. They would claim revenge, not understanding that she couldn't save both men.

If the men's injuries had been reversed, would she still have chosen Javier?

Probably, because her heart was tired of evil triumphing over good. She was desperate to put a win in the column for her team. Justice had been served to the one man who had tried to kill them, even though she wasn't supposed to be the one who determined who lived or died. Now she felt guilty about feeling all those things.

Which was why she could never be a murderer. Why she had turned Seth in to the police.

The guilt of not doing something against evil would have killed her first.

That's the one thing she wished everyone knew.

NINE

Kyle paced the hall. There was too much waiting in hospitals. They were back at St. George Regional. WIT-SEC thought it best to keep their resources concentrated in one place. Rachel was across the room in a chair sipping watered-down cafeteria lemonade. Javier had been evaluated in the ER. Rachel getting praised for saving his life. She did still hold her medical license from Boston, which probably protected her from liability. Though, from a past case he'd been involved in that dealt with medical malpractice, he knew you had to prove both negligence and harm to get a payout. A medical provider could be negligent, but if they did no harm to the patient, there was no case. And vice versa. There could be harm in a patient outcome, but if the provider hadn't been negligent, it was the same outcome.

Could he say the same thing about himself right now? He was being negligent in his duties as a WIT-SEC inspector. There was no doubt about that. He was emotionally involved with a witness, and it was clouding his judgment. If he stepped back and analyzed the case from the point of emotional detachment, there were several things that a curious inspector would have seen as red flags concerning Rachel.

One was her overall insistence that she had known nothing about Seth's crimes. Of course, anyone could look back with twenty-twenty lenses and analyze things now that should have been apparent then. Most spouses whose significant others were of the deviant type went through that process. However, the number of bodies that Seth had piled up rivaled the most prolific serial killers. Could she have been so enamored by his life-style and wealth that she'd ignored those red flags? Of course, it was plausible. That was human nature.

Denial was the specialty of humanity. Particularly when getting something that someone felt was missing from their prior life. It was hard to give up wealth after experiencing its advantages.

Second, there were the murder boards. That had left him unsettled since the first moment he'd laid eyes on them. A reasonable explanation was that she felt guilty and had wanted to make amends for not acting sooner on the things that she should have. But if he were honest with himself, it felt more than seeking justice. It felt like an obsession.

Third, her DNA at a crime scene when Seth was imprisoned. Had Penelope Schmidt been kept alive since the time she'd gone missing? Or had her body been stored in such a way to prevent decomposition? The medical examiner hadn't ruled either way at this point. Was Rachel the true criminal?

Though rare, there had been female serial killers. The brutality of the crimes lent to a male persuasion. Women tended to be cleaner when they were involved.

Even if they used a weapon like a gun or knife, torture was rarely involved, as it had been in Seth's crimes. Women didn't hold victims for days unless there was perhaps a monetary payout. Something like caring for an elderly person while establishing a way to cash in on retirement money and then doing them in. Most likely, if Rachel was involved, she and Seth had worked in partnership. That was more common in the literature. If that was the case, was she still fully under his spell and had he been directing her from prison?

He neared a window, pulled out his phone and dialed Gage Carter. "Hey, it's Kyle."

"How's Javier doing?" Gage asked.

"Should make it," Kyle said.

"I guess he's fortunate, considering who treated him in the field." Another reminder that most in WITSEC didn't consider Rachel's hands clean.

"When's the last time we inspected Seth's communications?" Kyle asked.

"Considering the developments in the case, we're poring through them as we speak."

"Anything unusual pop up?"

There was a shuffling of papers on the other end of the line. "About one year ago, it seems Seth was using a code."

"A code?"

"The letters are written in normal fashion, but at the top and highlighted in different colors for each correspondent is a code made up of numbers of letters. There are three different codes. Likely, the notes have something embedded into them, and the top code is either instructions on how to decipher it or it directs who it should go to," Gage said.

"Has anyone broken it yet?"

"Too soon. We're trying to gather more samples."

"What about his phone calls?" Kyle asked.

"Seth is a more prolific letter writer. He only calls one person, and that's Mommy dearest—who, of course, still believes in her son's innocence."

"Mothers usually do."

"What's your plan?" Gage asked.

"I'm trying to track down Dr. Nora Allen. Evidently, she hasn't been seen in a few days."

"Correct. Missed a few days of scheduled interviews. We sent some agents over to her place, but nothing seemed amiss. No signs of foul play. She took what a woman would normally take for a trip. Packed a bag. Purse, car keys and vehicle were gone. She's made regular charges to her account, so someone is using her credit card. Without other evidence of foul play, we're not going further with an investigation. Many people are upset that you would even consider that she's involved in criminal activity. She's a lot more liked around here than you are. She's not beholden to us to tell us every move she makes."

That stung, but it was the truth. Kyle's defense of Rachel had put him in the clear minority.

"You can't afford it, Kyle. The witness you lost— even though she broke WITSEC rules—is a mark against you. You should have been monitoring Rachel more."

"They may have their own life to some degree," Kyle argued. "They're not criminals."

"At least not criminals that have to go to jail. Come on, Kyle, you know quite a few people who we've had in WITSEC have not been the most trustworthy individuals. We've had felony murderers."

"And if so were ordered by the court and served jail time."

"Yeah, in our posh private facility to keep them out of gen pop, or even a private cell with a guard who might want to pervert his own justice. Listen, Kyle, I like you, but I see how your mind is getting fuzzy, and I'm trying to help you, as a friend. Rachel was in communication with Heather Flores. She had contact with her sister. Whether this break-in during her stay with her sister accounts for her DNA being present on the latest victim is yet to be seen, but you've lost your objectivity. You need to, one hundred percent, maintain professional distance. You cannot get wrapped up with this woman. If you do, it wouldn't surprise me if you became a victim yourself."

"Point taken."

"You're a good man, Kyle. You *cannot* trust her. You need to keep your head on a swivel, as they say. Watch your back."

As he looked at Rachel across the room, he didn't know if his heart could abide by what his mind and professional ethics dictated must be done.

Rachel could see Kyle's distress oozing from every pore. He paced and frowned. Whomever he was talking to intensified his mood for the worse. She was losing him. Not in the relational sense. One kiss didn't signify a liaison, no matter how much she wanted to explore it.

She was losing his trust. If a physical thing could represent an emotional change, then he was slowly building a brick wall between them. A strong one that she didn't know if she could break through. Even Rachel could see how guilty she looked, despite what she knew in her heart.

He disconnected the phone and paced toward her but stood a good three steps away. Too far away to have any intimate conversation. She stood, reached her hand out and placed it on his chest. "I'm sorry about your friend."

He grabbed her wrist and removed her hand from his body. "He wasn't my friend, but I appreciate the sentiment." He raked his fingers through his hair. "Rachel, I owe you an apology. I never should have allowed physical contact between the two of us. Nothing outside what is necessary for protection. It was irresponsible of me." He inhaled deeply and let the air slowly escape from his lips. "I must maintain my professional perspective. You can see how not operating that way puts all of us at risk."

Rachel's heart caved. She briefly glanced down to her chest to see if an open wound existed. The pain was so real. She was alone again. The trust she'd put in Kyle felt tainted. Perhaps men didn't change.

Rachel folded her arms over chest. "I understand."

"Do you?"

She bit the inside of her cheek, hoping the pain would dissuade the tears from falling. It didn't work. Rachel swiped at the tears and came up with a different reason for her emotional distress. Anything to keep from admitting the truth—that his words had wounded her, and she didn't know how many more inflictions she could take. Death by a thousand cuts. An emotional demise could still lead to a physical one.

"I'd like to see Heather before we go."

Kyle looked at his feet, shuffled them from side to side. "Why?"

"To check on her. She is a friend—my only friend."

Kyle's eyes widened at her statement. Briefly his lips parted, but a refutation of her statement was not forthcoming. He relented rather than argue with her. "For only a few minutes."

They walked to Heather's room. Kyle ushered her in but stayed outside to talk with the police officer who was standing guard near her room. It would be hard for WITSEC inspectors to cover a witness 24-7, and their resources were likely stretched thin with the Black Crew being so active.

When she first entered the room, Heather was sleeping. Rachel pulled up a chair and sat down, first noting the IV fluids that hung, how much oxygen she was on and how much blood still drained from her chest tube. These would likely be the same things Inspector Armijo would have after his surgery.

Rachel laid her hand over hers, comforted by the warmth—not feverish, which was a good sign.

Lord, we're alone, Heather and I. There's no one we can trust except for one another. Even those fighting to protect me don't believe in my innocence. Please, bring Heather back to full health. She has already endured so much pain and trauma. Don't let this event sideline the progress she has already made. She loves You. Please make it clear to her You love her just as much...

She'd whispered the words in her mind, but at the

end, Heather turned her hand and gripped Rachel's. "Why are you here? You know it's not safe."

Rachel smiled and gripped her hand back. "There was an incident at my grandmother's cottage. I probably can't ever go back there. The Black Crew shot an inspector. They transferred him here."

"Will he make it?"

"I think so...hope so. How are you feeling?"

Heather struggled to sit up. Rachel stood and used the bed controls to get her into a more upright position. Heather leaned forward, and Rachel instinctively adjusted her pillows behind her. Heather sank into the fluffiness.

"You should have been a nurse," she said, motioning for her water cup.

Rachel grabbed it and helped guide the straw into her mouth. "No. I don't have the patience that nurses do. I'm fine with a shorter interaction and having them do all the heavy lifting."

A knock came at the door, and a nurse walked in.

"Your ears must be burning," Heather said.

"Really?" the nurse replied.

Rachel checked the clock. It was two in the afternoon. Ward nurses usually made rounds at eight, noon, and four o'clock.

"Where's the nurse I had this morning?" Heather asked.

"Late lunch break. I'm bringing you your medication."

Rachel's heart settled a bit until Heather spoke.

"I didn't think I had anything scheduled until this

evening." Heather sat up more and straightened her sheets, bringing out her hand that contained the IV port.

"What medication?" Rachel asked.

"Um…an antibiotic. A new one."

Strange. Most antibiotics were hung as a piggyback, in a small bag, to an existing IV solution.

"What's the name of the medicine?" Rachel pressed.

The nurse eyed the syringe, and Rachel did so with equal scrutiny. It didn't bear a patient label. She took in the nurse's attire. The whole outfit came across as trying too hard. New scrubs. Starched to perfection. These days, nurses typically had a more laid-back vibe. It was almost as if someone was trying to exude what they thought the perfect professional nurse would look like in order not to draw suspicion.

His badge was turned around, so she couldn't read the name. "Can I see your badge?" Rachel asked him.

Heather reached out and took Rachel's hand, squeezing it tightly as a warning. Heather always was kind and loath to be embarrassed. "Rachel, I'm sure it's fine. There aren't boogeymen around every corner. We're in a safe place. There's an officer right outside my door."

The nurse turned it over and showed it to her. The photo was covered by a sticker of Kermit the Frog. More appropriate for pediatrics than an adult unit. Some nurses did this when they didn't like their photo or wanted to protect their information, but the badge looked worn, and the sticker was new.

"Heather, what was your nurse's name this morning?"

"Tyler."

It was the name on the badge.

"Male or female?"

"Female."

The interloper abruptly took Heather's hand and connected the syringe without cleaning it with an alcohol wipe. An infection-control no-no.

This wasn't a nurse providing care for her patient. It was attempted murder.

"Kyle!" Rachel yelled, and in the same second she slammed one foot on the pedal to unlock the bed while her other plunged into the side of the bed, sending it into the perpetrator's midsection and knees and knocking him down. The man righted easily and stomped back to the bed and grabbed for the syringe. In one motion Rachel reached over and ripped the IV out of Heather's hand.

Kyle broke through the door without hesitation and drove the man into the ground. "What's going on?"

"The syringe. You need to test it immediately. He tried to poison her."

Suddenly, the man laughed. A maniacal, mind-altering heckle. "None of you are safe. We're going to keep coming and coming and coming."

TEN

There was a full-force war in Kyle's body between his heart and his mind. He knew what everyone else believed about Rachel, but she'd also saved the last two victims—even himself and his more minor injuries— that had nearly been killed by the Black Crew. How could this amount to her working on Seth's behalf?

The intruder in Heather's room had been detained by the local police. They found Heather's nurse—whose badge the perpetrator had stolen on the outskirts of the hospital grounds—alive but severely beaten. Most often, smokers couldn't be close to the hospital these days, particularly staff, and it had been an easy opportunity for the man to knock the nurse unconscious and steal her badge to give him access to Heather's room and prevent questioning from the trained officer who sat outside the door.

The syringe had contained a combination of a paralyzing agent and Valium. At least in that way, the assassin had tried to be kind. Heather would have slept through suffocating to death. It still surprised Kyle that he'd taken the chance with Rachel in the room. Maybe

he'd also had plans for Rachel that hadn't come to fruition. A happenstance he would have acted upon.

Or the Black Crew was continuing to frame her. If
Heather had died in Rachel's presence, it would have
added to the belief that she was Seth's accomplice and
not simply his unknowing ex-wife.

Both stood outside the interrogation room, on one
side of the two-way glass, where the nurse impostor
sat, waiting to be questioned. None of the Black Crew
members that they captured had been willing to talk.
It would not stop Kyle from trying.

He faced Rachel. "Are you okay? You've said little
since we left the hospital."

"Is there anything to say?"

They were alone. The other officers were doing business elsewhere.

He knew what she meant without expanding on her
words. Maybe there was nothing else to say to her right
now. His words had been clear. She understood them
and was shielding her emotions in the same way he had.

Which meant there had been emotions to guard on
both sides.

"I'm going to go back to the hospital," Rachel de-
clared.

"For what reason?"

"I want to spend more time with Heather…while
it's legal."

"You'll need to be escorted," Kyle said. He turned
to the officer standing nearby. "Would you mind taking Ms. Bright back to the hospital and staying with
her? I'll come relieve you after I talk to this character."

The officer agreed. Kyle tried to meet Rachel's eyes,

but she turned to leave. An ache settled in his gut. The sensation troubled him. He was clearly falling for her. Thoughts of what life could be like with her had crossed his mind more times than he could count. Was there a way for them to be together? Could they come through something like this and be able to fully express what they both were feeling? Kyle closed his eyes. He did believe in prayer, though he didn't utilize it as much as he should.

God, this feels like an impossible situation. Bring Rachel and those she loves safely through this situation. I'm so afraid of losing her. If there's a way for us to be together, help us find it.

Kyle opened his eyes, turned the knob and entered the interrogation room.

This was what he could do right now to try and help Rachel. The other things were out of his control. He had to trust God was watching over those details.

Watching over Rachel when he couldn't be with her.

The assailant was tall, muscled, his body used to spending time in the gym. Shock of red hair. A smattering of freckles across his face. Fair skinned. Dark brown eyes. Not someone who blended into a crowd easily. Kyle dragged the metal chair out from the table. The shrieking sound as it scraped against the floor unsettled his nerves. It was the first time Kyle had felt the paranoia that his witnesses dealt with every day. When you didn't know who to trust and there were villains around every corner.

The man was a no-name to law enforcement. Cody McHale. No priors. Had never been arrested or charged with so much as a speeding ticket. His primary residence was in Boston, and he worked in pharmaceutical sales, which could explain how he became, presumably, closely connected with Seth—and likely explained his access to the medications he had brought with him to the hospital.

"I'm US marshal Kyle Reid."

"Marshal." The man returned Kyle's statement with an awkward, mocking salute. Attempting to raise one arm while simultaneously forgetting his wrists were handcuffed together. Trying for bravado. Coming across as a clown.

Kyle showed his badge. "I work in witness protection, and you're coming after my wards. I don't like it."

The man brought his well-defined arms to his eyes and mocked rubbing them—like a mime mimicking crying. "So, so sad." He slapped his hands onto the table. It took everything within Kyle not to jerk back. "Too bad I didn't get her. But as Seth says—we'll die trying."

Kyle crossed his arms and eased back into his chair. "Why do you follow him?"

"Why not? We're setting him free. An innocent man has been wrongly charged. It's about time he gets justice."

"Why would you want a serial killer out of prison?"

"So he can do as he wants."

"You're fine with him killing innocent women?"

"Someone has to thin the herd."

Kyle groaned inwardly. "You see the dichotomy here, don't you? You've just said you want to release an innocent man, but you know he's guilty of his crimes."

"All depends on how you define murder."

It didn't happen often, but there were truly evil people who wanted to see mayhem happen. It seemed Cody was one of them. It was the thing that fueled Kyle's belief in God—the balance between good and evil. The world was full of opposites, and one could not exist without the other.

"You would ruin your life for this ideal? You'll be brought up on attempted murder charges. Plus the assault on the nurse whose badge you stole. There were witnesses to your crime."

"If Rachel's believable, that is."

"What's that supposed to mean?" Heat flared in Kyle's chest. His hands fisted in his lap. Some days it took every rational cell not to physically strike out.

Cody smiled coldly. "I think the tide is turning against your most favored one. You seem to be only one of a few who believe in Rachel's innocence." He slid the handcuffs over the table. Kyle's skin prickled. "Some say she's a wolf in sheep's clothing and you're too blind to see it. You might want to beware. She ultimately could be setting a trap for you."

Kyle swallowed hard. It unnerved him, to be honest. Evil could more easily identify evil. It was a kinship. A look in the eye recognizable when you contained the same characteristics. Good people could more easily be fooled—because of their nature, they sometimes didn't buy into the twisted essence that could be the human heart. Was Kyle being foolish to continue to believe in the possibility of Rachel's innocence? Was he the only one who could see her goodness?

"You'll be going to jail for a long time. I'm wondering if you checked the state statutes," Kyle said.

"Meaning?"

"Massachusetts doesn't have the death penalty, but that's not true for Utah. The view on criminality here is a little different from out East."

"You're saying I could get the death penalty," Cody tried to verify.

Likely not, but that wasn't something that Kyle was obligated to share with McHale. Law enforcement could lie to a witness. He'd been read his rights and declined an attorney. For now, Kyle was well within the scope of the law to try to scare him a little into confession.

"You said it, not me."

The man inhaled sharply, contemplating his choices. Kyle used silence to let him sit and ruminate through them. One weakness of people was that they talked too much. Silence could be just as easy a generator of truth as pounding a suspect with a tirade of questions. People didn't like silence and would intentionally or otherwise fill the gap. Sometimes the information was useful—other times not.

"What if I helped you?" Cody asked.

Kyle leaned forward. "Depends on what kind of help you're offering. It would have to be a big help to take something like the death penalty off the table."

"What if I gave you inside information?"

"Depends on how significant it is."

"I don't mean inside information regarding what you call the Black Crew. Selling them out would easily mean my death—even in prison. I meant inside information about your highly esteemed organization."

Kyle leaned in. "That would be significant. If you expose a mole inside WITSEC, I can promise you it would be beneficial to any judgment handed down against you."

"I thought so. Wouldn't look good if someone on the inside was developing hit lists for those you're duty bound to protect. Right?"

"If proven true, of course," Kyle countered.

"Have you ever wondered how your two past locations have been disclosed? I mean, a grocery store in the middle of nowhere and a house Rachel was gifted that she thought was under the radar."

"Of course. But I didn't even know those locations myself. Nor did anyone inside WITSEC."

"That is, until you arrived there. Correct?"

Kyle stood and paced the room. Cody's deceptive language was a ploy, but hidden in the puzzle he was trying to weave was the clue Kyle needed to latch on to. Then it dawned on him. He exited the room and made his way to the parking lot, breaking into a run until he came to his car. Winded from the sprint, he got down on all fours and looked under his vehicle.

It didn't take him long to see what he feared was present.

A tracker on his vehicle. Likely placed by someone back at WITSEC before he had left to meet Rachel in Springdale.

There was one man Kyle could think of who would do that. Kyle grabbed the tracker and stomped it until it fractured, got into his car and hightailed it back to the hospital.

What was it they said? It was easy to continue to break a moral boundary once someone had surpassed it the first time. If so, Rachel was living up to the saying. She stood at the nurses' station in the ICU. It had been her intent to come back and visit someone, and she would stop by and see Heather again. It might be the last opportunity she'd have. But that wasn't her primary intention.

Her real reason was to visit Inspector Armijo. Something about him—his persona, his mannerisms, his looks—had bothered her ever since he'd set foot in her grandmother's cottage. Now it was time to see if her suspicions were warranted.

Peering through the glass window of Javier's room, she didn't see any medical personnel in attendance. The officer seemed fine taking a seat in the hallway for her to go in and have a private conversation. Without knocking, she breached the door and quietly closed it behind her. His eyes were closed—likely facilitated by a painkiller. Rachel stepped to his bedside and checked the medical equipment, just as she had in Heather's room. Basic IV fluids, a morphine drip and oxygen delivered through nasal prongs. His vital signs marched by on his patient monitor. Heart rate slightly elevated. Oxygen level normal, though on the low end. Perhaps the perpetrator's bullets had done more damage than she had initially thought. It was definitely plausible.

Rachel smoothed her hand over his until he opened his eyes. He startled and jerked his hand away. She pulled up the wooden chair and sat down next to him.

"How are you feeling?" Rachel asked.

"Better. Obviously thanks to you," he said, gathering the bed linens closer to his chest. "Can't say having this tube in my side is any fun—" He coughed, covering his mouth with his hand. Coughing was the result of the chest tube irritating the lung lining. It echoed Rachel's feelings "Happy to be alive, considering how far away the hospital was."

"When did Seth first come to you with his proposition?" Rachel asked.

"I have no idea what you're talking about," Armijo replied.

Rachel nodded. "About seven years ago, your daughter was severely injured in a car accident. She would have died without Seth's help, isn't that correct?"

The man remained silent, but Rachel could see he swallowed heavily multiple times in a row. A sheen of sweat broke out on his hairline. She was close to the truth, and she would pull it out of him. An ER physician was just as good as any law enforcement officer at getting the truth from a person wanting to keep it hidden.

"I almost didn't recognize you," Rachel said. "People look so different in a hospital setting—particularly when a loved one is close to death. It was both your wife and daughter, right? I'm sure, in your memory, I'm just one of the many medical personnel you crossed paths with. We all blended together. People rarely remember the first person in the hospital who comes to assist them. Usually they remember the one credited with saving the life, even though all the people along that path had a hand in it. But I digress."

Javier reached for his nurse call button, and Rachel tugged the cord to pull it out of reach. She would not allow him to signal for help to get out of this conversation. He then pulled the oxygen from his nose, and Rachel watched his numbers tick down. The ploy was a

Get up to 4
FREE FABULOUS BOOKS
You Love!

To thank you for being a loyal reader we'd like to send you up to 4 FREE BOOKS, absolutely free when you try the Harlequin Reader Service.

Just write "YES" on the Loyal Reader Voucher and we'll send you 2 free books from each series you choose and a Free Mystery Gift, altogether worth over $20.

Try **Love Inspired® Romance Larger-Print** and get 2 books and fall in love with inspirational romances that take you on an uplifting journey of faith, forgiveness and hope.

Try **Love Inspired® Suspense Larger-Print** and get 2 books where courage and optimism unite in stories of faith and love in the face of danger.

Or **TRY BOTH and get 2 books from each series!**

Your free books are completely free, even the shipping! If you continue with your subscription, you can look forward to curated monthly shipments of brand-new books from your selected series, always at a discount off the cover price! Plus you can cancel any time.

So don't miss out, return your Loyal Readers Voucher today to get your Free books.

Pam Powers

LOYAL READER
FREE BOOKS VOUCHER

◀ DETACH AND MAIL CARD TODAY! ▶

YES! I Love Reading, please send me up to 4 FREE BOOKS and a Free Mystery Gift from the series I select.

Just write in "YES" on the dotted line below then return this card today and we'll send your free books & gift asap!

➡ YES ⬅
- - -

Which do you prefer?

☐ **Love Inspired® Romance Larger-Print**
122/322 IDL GRCU

☐ **Love Inspired® Suspense Larger-Print**
107/307 IDL GRCU

☐ **BOTH**
122/322 & 107/307
IDL GRDJ

FIRST NAME

LAST NAME

ADDRESS

APT.#

CITY

STATE/PROV.

ZIP/POSTAL CODE

EMAIL ☐ Please check this box if you would like to receive newsletters and promotional emails from Harlequin Enterprises ULC and its affiliates. You can unsubscribe anytime.

Your Privacy – Your information is being collected by Harlequin Enterprises ULC, operating as Harlequin Reader Service. For a complete summary of the information we collect, how we use this information and to whom it is disclosed, please visit our privacy notice located at https://corporate.harlequin.com/privacy-notice. From time to time we may also exchange your personal information with reputable third parties. If you wish to opt out of this sharing of your personal information, please visit www.readerservice.com/consumerchoice or call 1-800-873-8635. **Notice to California Residents** – Under California law, you have specific rights to control and access your data. For more information on these rights and how to exercise them, visit https://corporate.harlequin.com/california-privacy.

© 2022 HARLEQUIN ENTERPRISES ULC
™ and ® are trademarks owned by Harlequin Enterprises ULC. Printed in the U.S.A.

LI/LIS-622-LR_MMM22

HARLEQUIN Reader Service —**Here's how it works:**

Accepting your 2 free books and free gift (gift valued at approximately $10.00 retail) places you under no obligation to buy anything. You may keep the books and gift and return the shipping statement marked "cancel." If you do not cancel, approximately one month later we'll send you 6 more books from each series you have chosen, and bill you at our low, subscribers-only discount price. Love Inspired® Romance Larger-Print books and Love Inspired® Suspense Larger-Print books consist of 6 books each month and cost $6.49 each in the U.S. or $6.74 each in Canada. That is a savings of at least 13% off the cover price. It's quite a bargain! Shipping and handling is just 50¢ per book in the U.S. and $1.25 per book in Canada*. You may return any shipment at our expense and cancel at any time by contacting customer service — or you may continue to receive monthly shipments at our low, subscribers-only discount price plus shipping and handling.

If offer card is missing write to: Harlequin Reader Service, P.O. Box 1341, Buffalo, NY 14240-8531 or visit www.ReaderService.com

BUSINESS REPLY MAIL
FIRST-CLASS MAIL   PERMIT NO. 717   BUFFALO, NY

POSTAGE WILL BE PAID BY ADDRESSEE

HARLEQUIN READER SERVICE
PO BOX 1341
BUFFALO NY 14240-8571

NO POSTAGE
NECESSARY
IF MAILED
IN THE
UNITED STATES

good one. A monitor alarming would bring help, probably more quickly than a nurse call button. Rachel grabbed the tubing. He brought his hands up and tried to force her away.

"Put this back in your nose and let us have a reasonable conversation about your misdeeds. If you don't, I'll reach out to Seth myself and tell him you disclosed his location."

"That would be a lie."

"You think Seth cares about differentiating the truth from a lie? He only cares about killing. Just knowing you had a conversation with me will be enough to get you marked for death. If you cooperate with me, your reputation, the love you have for your wife and daughter—you might be able to save all of that, because once Kyle knows about this he's going to become unhinged. If you choose to testify against Seth, you'll be fortunate if they put you into the very program you've tainted."

Javier put the nasal prongs back in his nose and inhaled deeply, bringing his oxygen numbers back up.

"The suit and tie threw me off. When I first saw you, you were dressed in jeans and an old college sweatshirt with bloodstains. Flecks of blood in your hair. You'd beaten your family to the ER. They were being helicoptered in."

Armijo lay there frozen, unable to move past the truth spilling from her. No doubt his mind was petrified by the thought of the prison sentence awaiting him.

"Seth recognized your daughter's devastating brain injury and hastened her to the OR… We could barely lay hands on her. It's probably why you think I wouldn't remember you, but I remember your distress. That's not something any physician casts easily from their mind. The darkness that can swallow a whole being when the fear of death of a loved one grips them."

"If you think there's some grand confession coming from me, you're more delusional than I thought you were."

Rachel stood and walked to the window. "I've always found it interesting that the things we despise in ourselves are almost always the things we're guilty of. When I was overweight, I was always much more judgmental about those who suffered weight issues. Here I was, a physician, and I couldn't follow my own advice. I think it was the anger at myself that perpetuated the judgment. Hating the weakness in others I couldn't self-resolve."

"Cry me a river."

Rachel turned back to the bed. "But that's exactly what you did. You accused me of the very thing you were guilty of. You betrayed everything you stood for. Did it surprise you when the Black Crew shot you so indiscriminately?"

Armijo's eyes widened, as if he hadn't considered the possibility.

"The last thing I saw before I ran up the stairs was the red laser on your chest…not on Kyle's. On yours. Once you've fulfilled Seth's wishes, he disposes of you. Once you make a deal with the devil, he'll kill you in the end. Whatever promise of safety and security he gave you was all a lie. And it won't end. He'll keep coming and coming…and not just for you, but for your family. For the wife and daughter you think you're protecting by giving Seth what he wants. It wouldn't surprise me if they've already gone missing."

Armijo's heart rate ramped up, the beep on his monitor driving faster. "It's not true."

"What? That Seth would hold to his word? His work as a doctor was a cover. He didn't hold to those ideals. The Hippocratic oath was a joke to him. You merely need to look at what he's most proud of."

Tears streaked down his face, the realization of Rachel's words bringing forth the emotion he'd likely bottled up as a defense mechanism.

"I was broke when we were in that car accident. I'd gotten into some trouble. A few poor investments. My daughter was hospitalized for several months. Over that time, you get to know your doctors pretty well. Seth is very easy to talk to. I shared about our financial struggles. Concerns about paying her medical bills on a government salary. I disclosed I worked with WIT-SEC. Seth, seemingly out of kindness, finagled it so that most of our medical fees would be waived. If I promised him I would repay him at some point. Of course, I didn't know what he was. I thought he would ask me to raise money for a good cause, not betray everything I stood for."

"You didn't study Seth well enough. He's all about undoing people. What deal did you make?"

"He kept tabs on my career. I thought transferring out to the west coast would put distance between us but it played into Seth's hands."

"Did you recommend Utah as my placement?"

"It was a group decision."

"Did you force it so I'd be close enough to keep tabs

on? Did you recommend Kyle's transfer out to the west coast as well so you could keep a close eye on him?"

"Kyle volunteered for that himself, though it did help that I became his supervisor."

Kyle ruptured through the doors. "Rachel, are you okay?"

She nodded, and Kyle turned his attention to Javier. "Want to explain to me how a geotracker made its way onto my vehicle?"

Armijo sighed. "Can we first check on my family and make sure they're okay?"

An announcement came overhead. "Code silver. Code silver."

Rachel bolted for the door.

ELEVEN

"We need to go," Rachel said.

"What does the code mean?"

"Someone is brandishing a deadly weapon."

Kyle motioned her away from the door and tugged down the blinds. He reached for his phone and reported to 911. Once he disconnected, he neared Armijo. "Did you do this? Did you give the Black Crew Rachel's whereabouts?"

His mute response seemed an answer in itself.

"You're working with Seth Black, aren't you?"

"I'm not answering any questions without a lawyer present."

"Whatever happens, you'll be on your own."

"Kyle, we can't stay here in this room like sitting ducks," Rachel told him. "We need to leave now."

He positioned himself in front of her, opened the door a crack and then pulled Rachel through the opening. "Where can we go with a locked door?"

"Patient doors can't be locked. Med rooms will be badge access only. Most supply areas will have a door with a punch code. That only leaves restrooms."

"No, they're too small of a space. Easy for someone to shoot through the door and hit one of us."

The halls were eerily quiet. Rachel could hear doors closing and then slams against the wood. Staff barricading themselves into patient rooms, trying to protect what charges they could. Kyle pressed against the wall and motioned her to do the same. Rachel pointed to the ceiling, where the red Exit sign was.

"Then our only option is out of the building," Rachel said.

"Not ideal. I don't want to get trapped in a stairwell, but it may be our best option at this point."

Kyle peered down the hall, his heart hammering in his chest. The ICU was on the third floor, so they had two floors to go down. There was a distant scream, then the sound of two gunshots.

Whoever it was, the gunman was on their floor. Kyle reached behind him for Rachel's hand and pulled her to the stairwell door. Stopping before it, he paused. Rachel braced herself. As silently as he could, he opened it. That's when the piercing beep flooded the floor.

As Rachel feared, the door was set to alarm if badge access wasn't used. It was a security measure to keep patients from fleeing without being detected. In this instance, it was a beacon to their location.

Kyle pushed her to the front, and she scurried down the cement stairs. They were down one floor when the alarm signaled again, followed by a few bullets pinging against the walls.

"Keep moving. Faster," Kyle urged. He stopped to pivot, firing a few shots upward into the stairwell.

Rachel cleared another floor, Kyle coming up fast

behind her. The next door let them out of the hospital. They ran through. Kyle motioned her to hide behind a nearby tree as he waited for the gunman to exit.

When the door opened, Kyle had his weapon in position, ready to shoot. "Drop your weapon."

The gunman looked toward the sky, exasperated, but did as Kyle instructed. That's when Rachel felt a presence behind her, bringing his arm around her waist. Before he could get her body pinned, she dropped down and elbowed her assailant in the groin. The pain plummeted the man to his knees. Rachel scurried to pin him to the ground, her weight over his back, and saw that his exposed hands didn't hold any weapons.

Kyle pulled out a zip tie from his pocket and secured the gunman that had exited from the stairwell. Then did the same to Rachel's attacker, who curled into the fetal position as soon as Kyle had secured his wrists.

"Nice move," Kyle told her, resisting the urge to pull her into a hug.

"What do we do now?" Rachel asked.

"Stay away from anyone in WITSEC. Until I know how deep Seth's claws are into that organization, we can't trust anyone there. If Seth was able to turn a well-respected supervisor against us, who knows who else might have gone astray."

The flight from St. George, Utah, to Boston, Massachusetts, had been a quiet one so far. Kyle had disconnected himself from anything WITSEC could use to find him. He'd purchased burner phones for himself and Rachel. He was wholly alone, trying to keep someone alive with just his own skill set, and he didn't know if it would be enough. As he sat beside her on the plane, he prayed.

Lord, I need You to work through me. Give me the power, the insight, the knowledge to keep Rachel safe. Help me find who is at the center of deceit within WIT-SEC so it can be a trusted organization again. Bring Seth Black and anyone who has helped him to trial. I know we don't always see justice prevail here in our time, but for the sake of humanity, help me end the reign of this madman.

Before he left St. George, he'd secured enough cash to operate off the grid. There were one or two agents he did completely trust—inspectors he knew had turned down a bribe in the past—but he would not reach out for help until he absolutely needed to.

"I know you blame Javier for what happened. For the tracker on your car. For the assault on the hospital," Rachel said, breaking into his thoughts. "But people will do extreme things to protect their loved ones. If Seth hadn't saved his daughter after that accident and made Armijo feel like he owed him something on a personal level when he never did, this wouldn't have happened. It's Seth's manipulation that twisted him. Sometimes I feel like we shouldn't be so hard on people when they've been emotionally manipulated to such a degree that they don't even see themselves anymore."

He turned to look at her, assessing her. "Was that you? And how you feel about how others judge you?"

Rachel wiped the condensation from the plastic cup she held. "Even very intelligent people can be gullible. Self-deception is the strongest of all defense mechanisms. I'm not saying Javier shouldn't be held responsible for the things he did in abandoning from the ideal of his job to do the bidding of a mass murderer. But clearly there were mitigating circumstances."

Kyle stared at her in disbelief—that she could offer such grace to a person who had set her up to be killed. Upon their first meeting in Springdale, she'd been all about exacting justice. Now she seemed to want to deliver more grace than had been afforded to her. He thought through other witnesses he had worked with, and never had he protected one who had such a sense of forgiveness.

"I am amazed by you," Kyle said, the words slipping out before he could pull them back.

Rachel smiled, shyness causing her to drop her eyes from his. "I don't know why. You see things like this every day working in the justice system. People making choices they shouldn't be driven to by extenuating circumstances. People will do lots of wrong things to get control back over their lives."

"I'm amazed by your forgiveness. True forgiveness is rare. I think victims and their families say it a lot because it's the *right* thing to say. And they want to seem above it. But you can tell they don't mean it in their hearts. That if the one who perpetrated the crime against them left the courthouse at that very moment, they would be the first to attack them and seek their own vengeance. How do you explain it?"

"I was talking to Javier before you arrived about how I sensed he was involved in exposing our location. I said to him that the very thing we accuse others of we are often doing ourselves. Perhaps the opposite is true as well—the thing we also need the most is the thing we're most willing to offer someone else."

"What you want most desperately is for people to forgive you?"

She nodded, fighting back tears.

It made Kyle wonder—what did she need forgiveness for?

TWELVE

It was dark. Kyle had convinced Boston PD to help him enter Dr. Allen's house. They were at the front door to her posh brick home that sat on the outer edge of the city near the water. The smells of salt and fish were heavy in the air, thick. A hint of electricity charged the atmosphere. A storm was brewing off the coast, about to make its way inland.

Nora Allen still hadn't been seen, and Kyle's badge had done enough for the local cops to believe his story that she could be missing or otherwise suffering under some mysterious consequences. Her ex-husband, Theo Allen, had a key and insisted on accompanying them inside. Kyle allowed it if the man promised to not intrude on their search of the doctor's things. Theo okayed it if they were respectful and didn't trash the place.

Despite Javier's actions, Kyle knew his next steps would not be looked upon favorably by WITSEC.

It would be helpful to have the ex-husband there. Hopefully, he could help them gain access to some areas of Dr. Allen's life that she wanted to keep hidden.

Once inside, with a few lights turned on, they got a

good take on the posh interior. The home was valued at close to $10 million. Seemingly, the good doctor was earning a lot more than just her income from the Bureau of Prisons. Government employment didn't pay this well. From what Kyle understood of her divorce, she was paying her ex alimony and not the other way around.

Kyle walked slowly through the rooms, looking for anything that might be amiss. He'd seen no signs of forced entry as Theo had punched in the code to disarm the security system at the front door. Neither were there signs of a struggle inside. The home seemed to be in its neat and proper sentinel state. Nothing knocked over or out of place. Some houseplants were starting to wilt, indicating Nora had perhaps been delayed longer than expected—or might have been detained against her will.

It was risky involving the ex-husband, and Kyle couldn't disregard his training. Theo could be responsible for her disappearance. Statistics bore that possibility out.

Theo went up to the nearest shelf that housed several plants. "She'd never allow this to happen. These plants are more important to her than people. If she had planned to be gone for an extended period, she would have hired someone to come and take care of these."

"Can you check with any service she might have used?" Kyle asked. "See if she made arrangements? Even excellent companies have people who flake out from time to time."

"Won't be able to do that until morning. I can send a few emails, but I doubt they'd be checked until normal business hours."

Kyle watched Rachel walk through the space. It was important to have her perspective as well. Women picked up on different clues than men did. Also, if Seth was involved, she knew his habits. His modus operandi. She could be better than a seasoned investigator in that sense.

"Does Nora have a home office?" Kyle asked.

"This way."

They followed Theo up one level. Off the bedroom was a good-size room, perhaps an old, swank master closet that had been converted into a home office. Rachel lingered in the bedroom while Kyle sat down at the computer and powered up the screen. "Know her password?"

Theo nudged him off to the side and made several attempts, without success. Kyle tried passwords that were associated with previous Black Crew members. What opened the computer was Seth's birthday.

Not a good sign that Nora Allen's hands were clean.

He began a search of her files. Checked her sent emails. Nothing too incriminating there.

"You know, she has a safe. Want me to open it?" Theo asked.

Kyle didn't believe in good fortune. But then again, few partners had friendly relationships with their exes. Perhaps this was Theo's way of getting back at her.

"I'm surprised she trusted you with that information and that you still have a house key," Kyle said.

The man shrugged. "I gave her all the house keys she thought I was in possession of. Doesn't mean I didn't make a copy."

For what purpose?

"Were you keeping tabs on her?" Kyle asked.

"I was worried about her. About some of her actions. Her suing for divorce…well, it came out of nowhere."

"When did that happen?"

"She filed shortly after Seth Black's trial."

"Do you think she was involved with him?"

"I don't know if I would say him specifically. But she had an unhealthy fascination with the case…and maybe with him. It was hard for me to tell the difference."

What was it about evil men that entrapped others so easily? Kyle could testify that there was a hypnotic quality to them. He could feel himself persuaded by their arguments until his law enforcement background kicked in and snapped at his ear to pull him back to reality.

Behind him, the man lowered a lever that opened a compartment on the bookshelf. It never surprised Kyle the lengths rich people went to hide their money.

"Does anyone else in your family have this birthday? February 28?" Kyle asked, trying to verify a non-nefarious reason that Dr. Allen might have used that for her password.

"Not that I'm aware of. We don't have any children. Her parents' birthdays were in the fall. She's an only child."

Curiouser and curiouser.

"There's a stack of letters here. From the prison," Theo said, pulling them out from the safe.

Kyle took the stack from his hands. They were from Seth. This didn't bode well for Nora Allen keeping her professional distance from someone who could influence her to do harm to the witnesses.

Maybe she and Seth were two peas in a pod.

Kyle pulled out the most recent note. He found the code at the top. The letter was unusually bland. What he'd had to eat. What books he was reading. Certainly nothing incriminating. There had to be something here. Why would Nora keep these notes unless they meant something to her?

Rachel came into the office and laid several beauty products on the desk. "These are all Seth's favorites."

Kyle raised an eyebrow. "Meaning?"

"Seth was very particular about my perfume and the shades of makeup I wore." Rachel motioned to the pile. "Versace Bright Crystal was a must. In my line of work, I couldn't wear it. Aromatic scents can be off-putting to patients and…well, you only need to make someone's nausea worse once before you learn that lesson. He would insist on this scent whenever we would go out…and I hated it."

It didn't surprise Kyle. Criminal types wanted to control everything in their sphere of influence. Dictating what a partner wore, their hairstyle, their makeup, was an additional way of exerting control. Almost building a prison without bars.

Theo picked through the items. "These are not what she used to wear. It makes sense to me what Rachel is saying. Around the time of our divorce, there was a drastic change in her appearance. Here, let me show you."

Theo pulled up several photos on his cell. "This is about a year before the trial. She's blonde. Her hair and makeup are very…"

"Natural-looking," Rachel offered.

"Exactly. Almost what people consider California

chic. Airy. She wore more flowy clothing. Jeans. Casual slacks. With long, drapey tops. A relaxed vibe."

He scrolled through a few more pictures. "I took these a few weeks after our divorce papers were signed. We ran into each other by happenstance at a local coffee shop. Her ending our marriage was a surprise to me. I loved her…still do. Nora never fully explained to me what changed. Just kept parroting the words *irreconcilable differences*. Maybe there were slight changes before that."

"Like what?" Kyle asked.

"Almost as if she was trying to cast off the life we had lived to try on something that didn't fit her. When she first started working for WITSEC, it was all about helping the victims. She was burned out in private practice. Not that those people didn't deserve therapy—she just couldn't relate to the high-society nature of their problems, I guess. She was raised in a lower-middle-class community. She worked odd jobs to get through college. Her parents gifted nothing to her when they died."

"And then?" Rachel prompted.

Theo cleared his throat. "Nora wanted to take part in the very lifestyle she said she detested. Started seeking out invitations to high-society parties. Sought court with the Boston elites. Supported candidates that were oddly more lax on crime."

Kyle inhaled deeply. It didn't take someone with a law enforcement background to see what had happened. Somehow, along the way, Seth had sunk his hooks into Dr. Nora Allen. And WITSEC hadn't ferreted it out, and now they were going to pay dearly for it.

"And then this." Theo held his phone out at arm's length, and Kyle saw the photo of Nora after the divorce. The difference was striking, and it brought a heaviness to Kyle's chest as he put it into context. He couldn't help but realize it was as if Rachel and Nora had switched places in their physicality. Nora had dyed her naturally blond locks to a deep brunette with bold red highlights. Her makeup was gothic. Heavy eyeliner. Dark eye shadow. Bold red lipstick.

It was a mirror to the past and how Rachel had dressed at the trial. Once Rachel had been free from Seth, she'd almost assumed what Nora Allen had once looked like.

"Can't you see it?" Rachel asked.

"That she's become Seth's preferred type? Yes, I see it. Mind if I take these?" Kyle asked Theo as he gathered up the pile of letters, not really intending to leave them behind regardless of the answer.

"Of course. I still care for Nora. Do you think something bad has happened to her?"

"I think she's gotten tangled up with Seth Black," Kyle answered. "I know when women do that, it's not usually a good outcome. We need to figure out what this code at the top of the letters means. I think once we have that, it will give us insight into where Nora might be."

The evidence linking Dr. Allen to Seth shouldn't have been that much of a surprise to Rachel, but if she were honest, it was like tremors to her foundation. Was there no safe place? No entity she could trust? Was Seth's reach that far and wide that she'd be his prisoner forever even though she wasn't locked up?

She pushed her way out of the house to sit on the stoop. She needed to breathe, but the stifling air from the incoming storm wasn't helping her to calm down. Where could she live to get away? Antarctica? At least the air there would be crisp and cool.

Kyle and Theo parted ways after Kyle gave him some reassuring words about keeping in touch and giving him updates if they discovered anything on Nora's whereabouts. Kyle had almost seemed grateful for Theo's deceit. That he'd had a key Dr. Allen didn't know about. Some of her most secret information was still in his possession. He could go into her home any time he wanted, and she didn't know it.

Were men all that different? Or did each of them manipulate, just on a scale? Zero being the lies of omission. Many didn't even consider that lying—just intentionally withholding the truth to spare someone needless worry. The noble lie. Was there any such thing? Didn't a lie always harm someone, whether it was withheld or twisted out of some sense of altruism? Was a ten on that scale taking another's life? Obviously, most men didn't reach the level of her ex-husband, but did they still have the manipulative component to their genetic makeup?

Kyle sat next to her. "What's on your mind?"

"Probably things you don't want me to share."

"I want you to tell me even those things. Even if you think it will hurt my feelings. We can't move forward unless you're able to do that."

"You mean move forward as far as my case? Or as far as you and me?"

"Is there a difference?" he asked.

Evidently not to him, but there was a difference to

her. Maybe it currently explained the chasm between them. Kyle was fully back in professional mode. Those things that they had shared—clearly, he felt they were a slipup on his part. She wanted to break down the barrier between them but also didn't know if she had the strength, considering all the other things she was currently fighting. Like trying to prove herself innocent of murder.

The trait of an ER physician took the better of her. Forcing the truth out of reluctant people. Or maybe drawing out greater insight.

"Doesn't it bother you?" Rachel asked.

"What?"

"That Theo continues to manipulate Dr. Allen?"

"How is he manipulating her?" Kyle asked, drawing an evidence bag out of his briefcase and tucking Seth's letters inside.

"By hiding from her the key he has to her house."

"What if he did it because he cared about her and what was happening? Maybe it's his love for her that's the explanation behind his action. He noticed a change in her behavior and was keeping closer tabs on her. Isn't that something you might encourage a family member to do if they were concerned? We both know not every mental health issue warrants an emergency evaluation and inpatient treatment. What is the plan that you institute if they sent someone home who might have been having thoughts of wanting to hurt themselves or others?"

"A safety plan."

"And could an ex-spouse be part of that plan?"

"Depends on what their relationship was like. Does that patient trust them?"

"So, not so far afield, wouldn't you say?"

"Theo could sneak in any time he wanted to."

"But there's not any evidence that he did that." Kyle cleared his throat. "Rachel, each of us has our biases. A scope that is colored by our choices. By our life experiences. You come from the perspective that someone that you loved deeply was working every second to deceive you, and I think that makes it hard for you to consider that Theo might have good intentions for keeping that key. He still loves her and wants to look out for her, to keep her safe. He's willing to do that even though she broke up their home and marriage."

Was this so different from God? How many times had she read biblical accounts of entire populations of people turning their backs on God, and yet time and time again, He tried to get them to see that by allowing Him into their lives, they would be so much better off?

Rachel set her elbows on her knees and pressed her palms into her forehead, trying to stave off a headache. Her arm itched from the healing laceration. She could normally quiet these sensations while her body was busy, but now that her mind was engaged in heavy thoughts, it seemed as if all these nuances were flagging her psyche for attention.

Kyle was right, in one sense. Being an ER physician brought that to light. It always amazed her how a clinic-based doctor and she could have wildly different assessments of patients who were referred into the ER. It took a few years in medicine before she'd sorted it out. The clinic doctors operated from a well bias. They assumed that most patients weren't that sick and would do fine without a lot of intervention. She operated in the opposite—all patients were knocking on death's door until proven otherwise.

What Kyle suggested was that Seth had forever tainted her view of men and their motives. That was probably true, but had Kyle shown her any difference at this point?

Kyle placed his arm around her shoulders—seemingly to interrupt the quiet space, to focus her attention back to what he was going to say. "I think Theo's intentions are true. He's still in love with her and anxious about what's happened. The divorce came as a surprise. From my perspective, sure, it wasn't great of him to hold on to her key without her knowledge, but if it saves her in the end from being murdered, then his actions proved beneficial. They're altruistic. He's not using his access to harm her...only to help."

Was he? Or were his actions just a means to an end? Rachel swallowed hard. Was her mind so bent that she could not see the good in anyone? Particularly men?

"What's our next move?" Rachel asked.

Kyle tapped his briefcase where he'd put the evidence bag with the prison letters. "We need to figure out this code. I think once we break that, we'll be able to get insight into where Dr. Allen might be and what Seth has planned."

They both stood and walked down the steps.

A white van accelerated to the front of the property. The door opened, and two men brandishing assault rifles pointed them directly at Kyle and Rachel.

"Ms. Black. Would you come with us, please?"

THIRTEEN

Kyle dropped his briefcase and went for his sidearm. The warning shot the assailants fired into the air halted his progress.

"Ms. Black. If you'll step inside." One of the men bowed to her and motioned with his arm to the inside of the van.

"She's not going anywhere with you," Kyle said. "You'll have to go through me first." He moved to position Rachel behind him, and they fired a round at his feet, chunks of sidewalk spraying his suit trousers.

"We don't mind doing that." The man snickered. "But Rachel could save your life if she merely came with us."

The men wore black ski masks. This seemingly had become the dress code for the Black Crew. This team was comprised of two men and the driver, who had waited patiently for this kidnapping to come to fruition. The exact moment when Kyle and Rachel would be alone. Kyle glanced sideways, trying to take in Rachel's demeanor. What he saw bolstered his spirt. Absent were trembling hands and tight shoulders. Instead, her jaw was set tight, and her nostrils flared.

Her body was priming for a fight.

"Ms. Black, we've asked you nicely two times now. Get into the van."

"I don't think your request meets the definition of *nicely* if you're holding a gun on us. You have fully removed the sense of choice," Kyle said.

"I'll give you three seconds," the man responded.

"These are the tactics you're going to use? How an adult would reason with a toddler?" Kyle responded.

"Fine. We'll pick a more adult choice. Rachel, if you don't get into the van right now, Mr. Reid, your proverbial knight in shining armor, gets a bullet. This time, not to the ground he walks on."

Kyle went for his gun but couldn't pull it in time. At first, he didn't hear the gunshot, but he felt the hot projectile slice through his flesh. The power knocked him backward into the brick steps. Blood seeped down his side, and he pressed his hand to the wound to stop the flow. The bullet had hit him on the lower left side of his abdomen.

When he had a moment to gain focus back on the street, he saw Rachel stepping inside the van.

"Rachel, no!"

He pulled his gun from his holster, pushing himself to a standing position and taking several wobbly steps into the center of the street as the van pulled away. No license plate. He aimed at the rear tires—and was rewarded when one of his bullets hit its target as the vehicle escaped into the night.

The punctured tire would stop them eventually, but

Kyle knew a lot could happen to Rachel in those moments. She could lose her life.

He holstered his weapon and got into his rental car, leaving a bloody handprint on the side. He pulled out his burner phone and called 911.

"This is WITSEC inspector Kyle Reid. I'm in pursuit of a white van that has kidnapped a woman by the name Rachel Bright, aka Rachel Black. I'm heading down Washington Boulevard—taking a right at Harrison. I'm in pursuit but am injured. Took a bullet to the gut."

Kyle sped up as soon as they were on a straight thoroughfare. The van took a hard left, and as Kyle whipped the car to turn the same direction, the seat belt dug into his wound and he cried out in pain. Perhaps it was more than just a flesh wound he was dealing with. Gunshot wounds to the belly were one of those things that rarely killed immediately but could take their toll over time.

His body shook and his mouth grew drier by the second. Shock setting in. Wet, bloodied hands made it hard to grip the steering wheel. The coppery smell of blood combined with the salty, humid air, nauseating him.

A nightmare was repeating itself. Another witness at risk of losing her life. It was more than his professional reputation at stake if Rachel died. His heart was at risk. Each moment he spent with her made it hard for him to imagine a life without her. He couldn't lose Rachel…not this way. Not on his watch.

She'd chosen to give up her safety for him. It had seemed reckless in the moment, her decision to step foot into that van. But if she hadn't, the gunmen would have had no compunction about sending more bullets his way to get her to comply. She'd had a decision to make, and she'd opted to save his life.

Who else did that remind him of?

Once inside the van, which reeked of marijuana smoke, Rachel was forced to sit in the back seat. The three men executed several celebratory, juvenile high fives, nonplussed that they'd just shot a federal agent. Kidnapped a woman.

Seeing Kyle down on the sidewalk, bleeding, yet still trying with all his effort to stop the assailants from taking her, tugged at her heartstrings. The look of terror in his eyes she'd seen more than a few times in her career.

That facial expression came when someone thought they were going to lose their loved one permanently. The depth of anguish was so pervasive it felt as if thorns of agony were being pushed deep in her soul. Rachel carried several of those barbs with her, and it was easy to recall the story behind each one.

Despite Kyle's words, Rachel could see she meant more to him than he alluded to. More than he was willing to expose at this moment in time. Would he ever risk it?

She turned away from her kidnappers and looked out the window. That was when she noticed there was something wrong with the vehicle. It tilted to one side and took a lot of handling from the driver to keep it between the faded street lines. Rachel glanced behind her and saw a set of headlights looming fast.

She prayed it was Kyle.

If Kyle was giving chase, his wound was likely survivable, though people could do amazing things with a cardiovascular system pumped full of adrenaline. Plenty of research supported that.

She needed time to figure out a plan.

Rachel flexed her fingers and cracked her knuckles.

The kidnappers' use of her married name was like a gnat buzzing in her ear. No matter how much she swatted at it, it just came back with its annoying high-pitched sound, aggravating her nerves to hysteria.

Just like Seth. He was unshakable and had likely insisted the kidnappers use Rachel *Black* for that very reason. He knew it would plunge a dagger into her heart. Signify, somehow, that he still had ownership over her. Show that he could exert control over her no matter where she was or who she was with.

Even if it was armed protection.

"What's the reward? What price is he willing to pay you to take me?" Rachel asked the kidnappers. She assumed the least threatening posture as possible. Legs crossed. Hands folded into her lap, though her fingers squeezed so hard together it was painful. It kept her from striking out when the moment wasn't opportune.

Certainly, Seth's family funds were helping their efforts.

There was a drag on the vehicle. The young men were eyeing one another, the driver revving the engine to get it to go faster. She could hear a car honking behind them. She turned and saw Kyle's face through the windshield. But he was not the one making the noise. It was the car behind him that was laying on the horn to get everyone to move faster.

"What's the reward?" one of the kidnappers yelled. "Infamy!" He pumped his fist into the air.

Unfortunately, Rachel knew that could be payment enough for some people. Just the minute possibility of having fifteen minutes of fame was enticing. Especially to this crowd.

"Where are you taking me?" Rachel asked.

"To see Seth."

Rachel's blood ran cold. No, this had to be avoided at all costs. Who knew what he would do with her.

"Might as well tell her, since she won't live that long, anyway," the driver said to the others, glancing at her in the rearview mirror.

His eyes had lost all semblance of humanity. Though pearlescent green, there was a dark shadow that overcast their luster. Something so heinous that it caused Rachel to tremble. It was easy to see evil in someone's eyes, and this man held copious amounts.

The one sitting next to her smiled knowingly. "It's all in Seth's letters."

"He's been writing to you?"

"Yes…for years. I mean, when you've got a life sentence, there's not a lot to do to pass your time. Have you seen the man lately? He's definitely using his one hour of exercise time and those prison steroids."

Rachel could hardly breathe. They hadn't answered her question, but it was clear Seth had been making plans and wasn't done with her yet. Not in any measure.

"That still doesn't explain how you knew where to find me."

"There's a code in his notes," the captor in the front passenger seat said.

"I know. I've seen it."

"You're a doctor, right?" the driver asked.

"Yes."

"Then you should know what it means. Seth always said it was a famous medical phrase. Something doctors say to patients every day in every hospital around the world."

Rachel searched her thoughts. The saying had to ubiquitous—even common to laypeople for these miscreants to know it. The young men were looking at her, motioning with their hands as if the movement would coax the saying from her mind.

She looked at the driver in the rearview mirror. Though he tried to hide it, he was struggling to maintain control of the lumbering van.

"You realize this car is dead in the water," Rachel said.

"It's okay," he said. "We only need to make it one more block for reinforcements."

Rachel's heart rose into her throat. She felt dizzy. She wasn't prepared to confront Seth. She'd gotten it into her mind that she'd never have to see him again, and she became madder at herself for buying into such delusional thinking.

"You better think twice about that," Rachel said. "You know there's a WITSEC agent who was targeted after he fulfilled his purpose for Seth, and then they went after his family. Everyone is still alive but suffering the consequences. Once you enter Seth's web, there's no leaving it."

"He'd never do that to us," the thug beside her said, laughing. Her skin prickled at the lack of understanding that the spider was bearing down on them as they struggled helplessly against the sticky, silky fibers.

Except they didn't even know they were entangled.

That was the most dangerous place to be. Just like with illness—some diseases were so silent that the patient could be weeks from death before they even felt ill. And then, if they were fortunate, it became a matter of—

"Two steps forward, one step back." Seth's favorite phrase came to her in a flash. That had to be the code on his letters.

"She got it!" The men set off more rounds of congratulatory pats on the back.

Rachel saw the flash of red on the traffic light ahead. Unfortunately, she also saw the driver's eyes were not on the road. A horn blared behind them, different from the earlier beep. This time it was incessant. She had no time to discern its meaning before the impact.

Glass shards sprayed onto Rachel's face. The back passenger door punched in as the van was T-boned at the intersection. The thug sitting next to Rachel, since he'd been unsecured, flew across her and was ejected from the vehicle through her window. He was tossed several hundred yards down the roadway, screaming wildly when he stopped. It was a reassuring sound, because he could at least take enough of a deep breath to wail. The van was forced diagonally across the intersection and slammed into a light post. The top of it came crashing down, indenting the roof of the vehicle. Rachel ducked, her breath quick in her chest. The assailant in the front passenger seat scrambled out as soon as the van came to a stop. Rachel unclipped her seat belt and lunged forward, wrapping one arm around the driver's neck and yanking him into the headrest to pin him.

"Don't even think about struggling," she whispered harshly in his ear. "You're going to thank me one day for saving your life, even if you think I'm trying to kill you."

FOURTEEN

After seeing the truck T-bone the van at the intersection, Kyle pulled his car to the side of the road. When he bolted from his vehicle, he stopped after a few steps to catch his bearings through the dizziness. He looked down at his drenched shirt. The blood loss was more impressive than he thought.

He staggered to the van. Rachel was still inside and had the driver in a chokehold to detain him. There was a young man screaming in the middle of the road, clearly suffering from two broken legs and who knew what else.

His priority was Rachel and making sure she was okay.

The window on her side was punched out. She and the driver were struggling, even though Rachel had the upper hand. The man attempted to bite her arm, clawing at the exposed flesh, and yet she remained steadfast with her hold. Kyle drew his weapon and pointed it at the driver.

"Put your hands on the steering wheel," Kyle yelled.

The driver did as instructed, and Kyle zip-tied each

wrist to the steering wheel to keep the driver contained, and then he fell down onto one knee. The back driver door opened, and Rachel knelt next to him.

Kyle shook his head. They were still in too much danger. The front passenger was on foot. The man could bring more Black Crew members at any time. Kyle worried about the man in the middle of the road even though he couldn't walk. Two hands could still hold a weapon and shoot. He got to his feet and walked toward the man in the street. A quick survey of his wounds lent toward survivability in his non-medical opinion.

"Let me see your hands," Kyle ordered. The man did so, and Kyle restrained them despite the man's moans of pain. After securing his hands, he patted down his body finding only contorted lower limbs.

Now his concern drifted to the one who'd fled the scene.

"Lay down, let me look at the gunshot," Rachel said.

"I can't stop until we find the passenger."

"Kyle, lay down," she ordered, just a hair under a full-on shout.

He acquiesced, and the cooling breeze of the night air kissed his skin as she moved his shirt aside. His thoughts were wandering away. His only focus was on her touch as she gently explored the skin around his wound.

"You've lost a lot of blood. It's probably why you're not feeling all that well."

She brushed the sweat off his forehead. It confused him how he could be drenched when he hadn't run after anyone—simply stopped his car and paced a few steps.

"The bullet might have nicked your spleen. Could

explain the degree of blood loss. Probably not too badly, since you're still with me."

With me.

The words were a solace. He could feel something within him slipping. Almost an unhinging of a deep connection he had with terra firma. He felt light and warm. Peaceful and calm. Whatever part of his soul connected to the physical was lifting its anchor.

"Kyle, stay here," she shouted at him. "We're not done yet. I need you. Hold your hands over the wound."

He popped his eyes open. Forced his vision to focus and find her eyes. His hands sloppily did as she asked. She brushed the fingers of one hand through his hair, then, with the other, reached for her phone to call for reinforcements. Her needing him was the one thing anchoring him back. All he could see was her eyes set against the faint, intermittent lights of the twinkling stars flirting with him from a distance. He turned his head, and she placed her palm on his cheek.

"Stay with me," she pleaded. "We've got a lot to do yet. A killer is—"

But the distant tug became too enticing, and he let himself drift away into blackness.

Rachel sat next to Kyle's bedside, holding the stack of Seth's letters to Dr. Nora Allen in her lap, deciphering them.

Seth's code was simple but devious. *Two steps forward, one step back.* The phrase tried to encourage patients that an upward, unbroken trajectory wasn't always possible with most injury and illness. But now the supportive phrase had been used as the cipher for a killer's devious plans.

Rachel had been right in her diagnosis of Kyle. The bullet had passed through his abdominal cavity but nicked his spleen as it passed, causing him to lose too much blood. At least the doctors didn't think the damage was extensive. They'd given him blood, and the staff would monitor his red blood cell levels overnight to ensure they were stable and likely send him home in the morning. Where they would go was an uncertainty. Kyle needed rest, though he would be loath to do so with Seth loose and a woman's murder unsolved—particularly when Rachel's life was on the line. WITSEC would probably afford him the time, but he wouldn't allow it for himself. Plus, how much did WITSEC know at this point? Kyle had purposely kept them off the grid, but surely this incident had risen to their attention.

Kyle's color was finally pinking up after his third unit of blood. His cheeks held a hint of red, his lips their normal color. His hand was warm when she touched it. The nurse had just disconnected his tubing and was taking her final set of vital signs to monitor for any adverse reactions from the transfusions. He roused as the blood pressure cuff squeezed his arm and saw Rachel sitting next to him.

He pulled the oxygen mask off his face. The nurse didn't make any moves to stop him, as his oxygen levels had been stable over the last several hours and now his blood levels should be near normal. Currently, he had enough red blood cells that he should be able to maintain a normal oxygen level. He rubbed his chapped lips together, and Rachel picked up the cup of water at his bedside.

"Drink?"

He gratefully took a few sips and then eased the cup away. "How are you?"

"I'm just fine other than the expected body aches. I'm not the one who took a bullet."

"It barely grazed me."

Rachel laughed. "I think your spleen disagrees."

When the nurse finished and left, Kyle pulled his covers off to the side, attempting to stand with his overly thin hospital gown barely covering anything. Rachel stood and placed two hands on his shoulders, easing him back down onto the bed.

"Sit down. Doctor's orders."

For once, he didn't argue. "Do we know anything?"

"I'm not sure about the men they apprehended at the scene. They've been detained. The police knocked on some doors around the neighborhood, but they didn't find Seth. It's not known if he was there or if the men who kidnapped me just thought he would be."

"I get the first crack at him," Kyle said.

"In your condition, there'll be no cracking in the short term. Good news is, we may not need him anymore."

Kyle eased back onto the pillows. "How so?"

"Those men who snagged me didn't think I was ever going to see the light of day again, so they gave me the clue on how to use the code written at the top of the notes to translate what Seth was trying to hide. 'Two steps forward and one step back.' It's a phrase we use in medicine all the time." Rachel held up one note. "See here." She showed Kyle one of the most recent letters Seth had sent to Nora. "I find the first letter as noted—go forward two and then back one and write those letters down."

"What is Seth trying to say?"

"I haven't gotten very far yet. I've only done the oldest and newest letters. Might not seem logical, but I wanted to see the last bit of info he might have been trying to convey to her and the genesis of how everything started."

"How did it start?"

"Nora was a woman looking to live on the wild side. She left a man who clearly loved her. There wasn't any evidence, at least from Theo's telling of their tale, of infidelity or even acrimony on his part. It seems Nora was the one who…felt unsettled. I think Nora reached out to Seth first."

"What?"

"And then joined WITSEC at his behest."

"When did that happen?"

"Keep in mind that Seth's trial didn't begin immediately. He was in jail for a good couple of years as they built the case against him. It was toward the beginning of his jail time. The first letter holds the code. No doubt Seth had used this phrase with her as a clue. It would seem innocuous to anyone who was listening. It's a common enough phrase."

"But how do you know she reached out first?"

"In Seth's first letter to her, he says as much. 'Thank you for contacting me.' Of course, he hides this in code, and it's not as well written as what I just said. It's choppy, but it's clear."

"Does he indicate why she reached out?"

"There are words like *research study*. Serial killers have always been a fascination. It's how the FBI started the Behavioral Sciences Unit. Trying to figure out the crimes from known serial killers to prevent new ones from cropping up."

"You think Nora's interest was benign at first, then?" Kyle asked.

"Unknown. To be honest, Nora was conniving in this way. Maybe a hint that her inner self wasn't as altruistic as she wanted people to believe. If she could be the first to get Seth's story and publish it—that would be more lucrative than even private practice for Bostonian elites."

"Is that conniving or just good business sense?" Kyle countered.

Rachel disregarded the comment. "I'm sure we'll know more as we go through the letters, but Seth's response to her inquiry probably sounded like, 'I'm misunderstood. Let me tell you my story.' Seth's cooperation would be too tempting to ignore, particularly for someone like Nora, who might have been looking to live on the dangerous side. I think her ex alluded to this when we met him. She wanted to be part of the upper echelon. Wasn't happy leading a quiet, homebound lifestyle. It wouldn't surprise me if Seth was reading the Boston papers for clues to his own case when he came across the society pages and saw a recurring theme of her presence. He likely, though maybe not consciously, recognized some of his own qualities."

"What does the last letter say?"

"It gives a meeting time. The letter was sent almost

three weeks ago, which is strange, because it means Seth would have had to know that the allegation of jury misconduct was coming. How could he have known that?"

"Good question." Kyle inhaled deeply and rested his head against the pillow. "There was an excellent judge on the case. The jury was sequestered during Seth's trial. In order to know that the jury member didn't disclose that she'd been a victim of violence, it would almost be that each one of them would have to be investigated. The court depends on a certain level of honesty. They don't have the time or resources to investigate whether jurors are being honest on their forms. Someone would have had to discover the fabrication and disclose it to the courts."

"Seth had a lot of time on his hands. A mind like his will not sit idle—it needs an outlet."

"We need to be at that meeting. It might be our only opportunity to get Seth. If he expects Dr. Allen to be there, we need to be there in her place."

Rachel fanned her face with the letters. "But where is Nora?"

"If she's wanting to live life dangerously, maybe she's the one who is framing you for murder."

"She and Seth could be together now, for all we know," Rachel said.

"They could be, but I'm doubtful. Seth might have her prove herself to know her level of loyalty. He could think she's still part of WITSEC. He'd have to convince her to do something illegal. Something he could hold over her to make sure she's totally under his thumb. If she does certain acts, he'll know for sure she's with him. My guess is when they meet, he'll make it clear that if she ever goes against him, he'll release the evidence he's holding against her and clarify that prison isn't a nice place to be."

"Mutually assured destruction."

Kyle reached his hand out to her, and she laid her hand in his. "It terrified me to see them take you. Don't do that to me again."

"Why did it terrify you?"

Kyle's eyes widened. She was pushing him to say words he was, perhaps, not ready to say. But she needed to hear them. She had no doubt there were growing emotions between them. She needed to know that what she was feeling was reciprocated.

"I can't lose another witness."

Her heart sank. A professional reason wasn't what she was hoping to hear. But she didn't let her disappointment show. "If I didn't go with them, they were going to kill you."

He gripped her hand, hard, and gave it a tug. Once her eyes met his, she saw the aching there. Something that held her gaze that she hadn't seen before. An inexplicable longing. "Rachel, your job is not to protect me. Your job is to stay alive…even if it means that I die. Promise me you understand this."

She slipped her hand from his. "I can't and I won't. You're asking me to go against every principle that I hold dear. An oath I swore to. Seth might have corrupted every word, but I take it seriously."

"Rachel, please, look at the greater good." Kyle sighed. "We have competing ethics, and I'm going to tell you why mine is more important. It's something law enforcement leverages every day. We let low-level bad individuals go free but get a bigger fish, knowing it might save more people. Trading in a drug dealer for a distributor."

"Kyle—"

"Before you say anything, let me get this out. Your life is more valuable than mine. We need you… *I* need you to stay alive. The world needs Seth to go back to jail. Who knows the influence he would have if he were free, especially now, considering all of his followers? If it comes down to it…you can't let that happen, Rachel. Promise me."

Rachel cleared her throat. "In medicine, each life is held in equal measure. We don't decide like that. The drug dealer suffering from the gunshot wound is treated as decisively as the mother of five suffering from a heart attack."

"You triage based on condition, right? The patient who will die first gets treated first."

"Right."

"Unless it's a mass-casualty incident, and then what happens?"

Rachel settled back in the chair. Kyle was as good as Seth. He was going to use her principles against her, twist them into something so she'd have to obey. This didn't feel good to her. Her heart wanted to acquiesce, but her thoughts were steaming. The same anger she'd felt at Seth when he would do this very thing to her.

"It's flipped. We look at our resources and treat those who are most likely to survive. If you're near death, you'll end up with a black tag on your toe. If there's enough, we might give you a little painkiller."

Kyle braced his side and sat up. "This is a mass-casualty situation for WITSEC. A bomb has gone off in our organization. I don't know how many witnesses are at risk. But what I do know is that if you die, then Seth will become an evil unleashed again—never to be contained. He'll have learned from his mistakes and won't get caught again. My life is worth trading to keep him behind bars. Yours isn't, because you're one of the few who can put him back there."

"Kyle…"

"Rachel, please, promise me."

She stood up and set the stack of letters at the end of his bed. "You're doing what Seth would do to me. You're asking me to trade what I hold dear for something I could never do. If I have any power, I'm going to work to save who I can. This isn't a mass-casualty situation. You're someone that I—"

What word was she holding back? *Admire? Like being with? Love?*

She bit her lip and backed away from him, trying to stave off her tears. He'd made it clear they couldn't be together. Now, he was asking her to let him die to save her own life.

The torment was splitting her in half. She did the only thing she could do. She turned and left the room.

FIFTEEN

Kyle waited outside the interrogation suite for them to bring up the driver of the van who was part of Rachel's kidnapping. How many times had he been in such a position over the last week? Seth's magnetic pull was impressive. To be able to convince a group of people to keep hunting another.

He hadn't seen anything like it in his career.

There were groupies and there were devotees. Groupies followed at a whim. They had adoration but likely wouldn't do anything illegal. A devotee was a different animal. They elevated their admiration to a religious zeal. It became a fever pitch and caused them to do irrational things. Manson had inspired this kind of devotion. Seth Black followed in his footsteps.

It had been two days since Kyle's hospital release. Three days since they'd taken Rachel. His stomach clenched as he relived her kidnapping. At least they hadn't gotten her to the final location. Motor vehicle collisions were never pleasant, but Kyle felt the hand of providence in this instance. If the truck hadn't plowed into the van and the kidnappers had gotten much farther, Kyle wasn't sure he'd have been able to save her.

Seth's underlings seemed to be escalating. So far, they'd been overcome, but Kyle couldn't depend on that to be the case with every contact. Each instance was becoming more deadly. It was probable that Seth had more competent people in his inner circle. It could explain why Dr. Nora Allen was still missing in action.

Kyle rubbed his hand over the stubble on his jaw. Until this crisis was over, there was only so much he could concentrate on and shaving was one thing he'd discarded. His left side ached. There was no denying the pain. It was difficult for him to walk upright. Unfortunately, he couldn't take anything that would cloud his thinking. Before WITSEC released him back into action, he'd had to prove he could physically protect Rachel. Running, climbing, shooting with accuracy. He'd been able to do those things—against doctor's orders. For the physical agility test, he had slipped one of the opiate pain killers the hospital had released him with. Since then, he'd been living on alternating doses of acetaminophen and ibuprofen, which kept the pain to a tolerable level.

Neither his medical team nor the government were happy about it, but when Rachel had insisted he stay on her case, that helped. WITSEC was all too eager to figure out if she was someone they needed to turn over to the law, or if there was a mole framing her that needed to be smoked out of his, or her, hole. Obviously, one over the other was better for their bottom line.

His musings came to a halt when two officers brought up the suspect. To describe their suspect as nondescript was an understatement. There were no unique features about him. He could have been anyone. He didn't look lonely—like someone driven to Seth's group because he had unmet, unidentified, deeply unresolved and thus unconscious issues. Essentially, someone who didn't know themselves and what they stood for. He was a married man with two children. Daughters, even. How could he see himself kidnap another woman and bring her to a certain death? He'd held a job—for several decades. Dedicated to his church—at least in action, though clearly not in spirit. No priors—not even a traffic ticket. What was it about Seth that could get a man like this to abandon everything he believed in?

Rachel was secured elsewhere in the building, being watched over by a member of law enforcement. He just couldn't have this man salivate over her presence while Kyle tried to get him to take part in a plan to trap Seth and end this crisis. Ultimately, proving Rachel's innocence and setting her free.

Once the prisoner was seated and secured, Kyle squared his shoulders and entered the interrogation room. He tried to walk, unsuccessfully, without leaning to his left side. The doctors had admonished him to take it easy. That if he physically exerted himself, the laceration to his spleen could start bleeding again, and if he wasn't close to medical aid, then he was risking his life.

Did it matter? If he didn't keep Rachel safe and prove her innocence, was life without her worth living?

The question paused his thinking. After he lost the prior witness, though it traumatized him, he still had hope and direction. He hadn't questioned his ability to carry on. Without Rachel, though, the very thing that was keeping him moving forward would be gone, and he couldn't bear to think about life under those circumstances.

Something about Rachel made him doubt his ability to go on alone. They were partners. She had saved his life just as much as he had saved hers. And maybe she was ahead on the keeping-tabs card. She had proven to be a woman that he could see himself abandoning this chaotic life for.

Kyle pulled out a chair and sat down at the table. Mr. Johnson was handcuffed to a chain bolted to the floor. A guard waited in the corridor, constantly peering in. Thus far, though read his rights, Johnson hadn't requested an attorney. Another strange thing about Seth's followers. Was it that they all thought they could beat the system? Few, if any, asked for representation, though the one sitting in the hospital bed with multiple fractures to his legs had done so the first moment he could speak. The other kidnapper who had escaped remained elusive.

"Brad Johnson, I'm Kyle Reid."

"I know you," the man said, his voice deep and full of bravado. "There's not a member of the Black Crew that doesn't know the infamous WITSEC inspector Kyle Reid. We study you like we study Rachel—maybe more so. If we know you and your movements, we can find her and bring her to justice."

The Black Crew had adopted the same principles as the Behavioral Sciences Unit. The thought wasn't comforting.

"Is that what you think you're doing? Helping Seth?" Kyle asked him.

"Of course. The man was wrongly convicted. It's been his wife all along. I hate to see innocent men go to prison or suffer the consequences of choosing the wrong women."

That could be what law enforcement missed. It was normal to run background info—the obvious things they knew in the short term. Rap sheet. Criminal history. Times contacted by the police. But marital history took more to delve into. Time and resources they didn't have at their disposal in the moment.

"You're married now. Two teen daughters. Seems like a good match. You've been together several years. Things not as they seem?" Kyle asked. Often, when law enforcement interrogated a witness, they feigned interest in a suspect's personal life to build rapport, but Kyle was drawn to these aspects like moth to flame. Brad Johnson's view on how devious women could be could have caused him to sidle up with Seth and make him more able to believe the lies Seth sold.

"Second marriage," Brad said simply.

"And how was the first?"

The man shrugged, trying to appear nonchalant, but his shoulders hinged up a little longer than what the gesture required for Kyle to believe the sentiment.

"Are you paying alimony to your ex?"

The man's hackles raised. Kyle had flipped a trigger. "Do you know what it's like to subsidize a woman who is physically and mentally able to take care of herself? Do you know what that payment takes away from me being able to provide for the family I have now?"

There it was. The tamped-down anger that slowly heated. It was near boiling under the surface. Now Kyle could easily see how Seth had lured him in.

"Did you ever take her back to court to change the arrangement of your alimony payments?" Kyle asked.

"I did…when my girls were young, but I quickly discovered what a scam the whole thing was. The only ones getting paid were the attorneys, and nothing was changing for me. I figured at least the money I didn't spend on attorneys could go to my children. I decided to stop for only that reason."

"Must have been tough to feel that…injustice."

"Have you ever been married?"

Kyle leaned back in his chair. "I haven't."

Johnson backhanded his nose to clear the secretions. His eyes glossed over. Kyle could work with this. "Imagine loving someone with your whole heart. Body. Soul. And then they turn on you in the most fantastically devious ways. The betrayal. The proverbial knife between the shoulder blades. It's as painful emotionally as if it had been done physically."

Strangely poetic for someone in his circumstances. Brad Johnson was an intellect. His language and mannerisms exuded this fact, despite his current financial state. Sometimes, morally minded people couldn't see past their convictions to be able to see when they were crossing a line.

His words were a picture frame for Rachel's life as he'd been led to believe. Only Kyle doubted that Brad's ex-wife had become a serial murderer. "I can't imagine it, but I know someone who has lived that life."

The man laughed abruptly. It was a jarring change

of emotion. Kyle jumped slightly. The momentary grin that crossed Brad's face unsettled him. "Don't for one minute try to claim you're thinking of Rachel."

Kyle took his advice. "How did you meet Seth?"

"Online. A support group for divorced husbands."

Kyle doubted that could be possible. They did not give high-risk inmates like Seth Internet access for this very reason. Plots could be made. Not just against others but escape plans to get out of jail.

"You were speaking with him directly?" Kyle attempted to verify.

"Not me, but another gentleman in our group was getting letters. They—"

"Contained a code."

Johnson's eyes widened. "You know about that?"

"There's little we don't know. Seth assumes we're in the dark about a lot of things. Just another thing he's misguided about."

That man inhaled deeply and mirrored Kyle's posture, clearly contemplating whom he wanted to believe in—the convicted psychopath or the member of law enforcement he'd studied for years.

"Why are you helping Seth? Why kidnap Rachel?"

The man fidgeted. Pursed his lips together as if giving himself a physical reminder to keep his mouth shut.

Kyle leaned forward. "This is going to come as a surprise to you, but you bet on the wrong horse. Seth isn't the innocent man he claims to be. Think about what he convinced you to do. He plied you with a story to get you to commit a crime for which you will go to jail. How will you be able to provide for your family then. Did you watch the trial?"

"I did."

"All those witnesses were wrong? You know the famous line—either Seth is guilty, or he is the most unfortunate man that ever lived to have so many people come against him. Coincidences just aren't that common, to tell you the truth."

"What about the most recent victim? Penelope Schmidt?" Brad asked.

"Convenient. Likely a frame job."

"And you don't think the same thing could happen to Dr. Black?"

The deference this man gave Seth churned Kyle's stomach. Seth was the very opposite of a healer. He turned people against themselves and incited them to do things that were detrimental to their lives. It was just another thing that was a thrill for him. People abandoning the truth for a lie. All part of his criminal psyche—to see how his words and actions could cause people to twist in the wind.

"It's easier to frame a person for one crime than it is to frame someone for fifty-plus murders. That's the number of bodies we feel Seth is responsible for, though not all have been found. At the trial, there wasn't any doubt among the jury that Seth was the true killer. No one wavered from calling him guilty on all counts."

"That's the problem. You're holding him responsible for crimes of which you have no evidence."

"The thirty women we found murdered aren't enough for you?"

Johnson looked askance. Kyle was breaking through the facade that the anger toward his ex-wife had made him gullible to. He moved his legs to stand up when he was reminded by the chains bolted him to the floor. If only he realized there was a yoke he carried that he'd placed on himself.

Kyle pressed on. "Why would Seth reach out to a bunch of wounded ex-husbands in a divorce group? He knows all of you have been scarred emotionally and can be plied by his words. Particularly if you are disgruntled with your ex, or the divorce settlement, or are not trusting of women any longer. How much does it take to call a man to action to right a perceived injustice when he's already biased against women?"

Brad dropped his head into his hands to hide his weeping.

"I can protect you from going to jail. I can probably even get these charges against you waived. You can return to your wife and family and go on living as you were before. Put Seth and this whole incident behind you. Few people get that chance. You can get out of this alive with a new lease on life…and maybe a new perspective."

"What do I have to do?"

"Help me set a trap for Seth."

Rachel teared up when Kyle pulled up in front of a nondescript hotel outside Boston. A gift had been given to her. Her sister waited in one of these rooms. Protecting Sofia was part of Kyle's elaborate plan to trap Seth. Rachel's doppelgänger, a WITSEC agent Kyle trusted, was lying in wait at Sofia's house and being very open about her presence with seemingly only one inspector protecting her—dressed as a beat cop. The hope was that Seth would take the bait and they could arrest them there. Rachel knew some of the plan that was designed to flush Seth out and hopefully discover what had happened to Dr. Allen. Kyle didn't discuss his thoughts on whether Dr. Allen was alive or dead.

Something had changed with Kyle. Not that he was any less stressed. In fact, he seemed more so. It was his demeanor toward her. He was soft with his words. Ever since he'd met with Brad Johnson, he'd seemed to want to make amends in whatever way he could, and allowing her to see her sister was part of it.

Sofia opened the door, holding Lyla in her arms. Rachel rushed through and crushed them both in a giant hug. The moment seemed surreal, and she didn't want to let either of them go until Lyla said repeatedly, "Auntie Rachel?"

"I brought you a gift," Sofia said.

"What? Why? Seeing you is the only gift I needed."

Her sister presented her with a small, wrapped package. "It's your birthday in a few short weeks. I didn't want to miss out on the chance when we've missed so many celebrations together." Rachel pulled at the paper, opened the box and saw a pair of peridot earrings. Her birthstone. They dazzled. She was mildly perplexed.

"You don't like them?" Sofia asked.

Rachel, who hadn't worn earrings in years, pressed them through her old holes, feeling a slight pinch as she did so. "They're beautiful. It's just that…you know I swore off jewelry years ago after I got that hoop earring ripped out of my ear by a patient."

"Which is why I chose the studs. You deserve something as beautiful as you are." Her sister fingered her earlobes. "They look great. You're stunning." She edged her back to arm's length. "The desert did amazing things for you."

Rachel gripped her sister's hands. "I brought nothing for you. I'm ashamed of myself."

Her sister locked eyes with her. "You should be." A shadow fell over her countenance. "Remember, things are not always what they seem."

Rachel's heart faltered. What a strange thing to say. Was Sofia trying to pass along some type of message? "Are you okay?"

Sofia took a few steps back, and they held one another with their eyes. Rachel tried to decode the meaning of her words as she waited for her sister to reply. Sofia never did. She merely pulled back Rachel's hair to show off the earrings.

"Doesn't she look amazing?" Sofia's question was directed at Kyle.

A flitter in Rachel's gut signaled alarm. Something was up with Sofia. A forced exuberance when her body language screamed her nerves were on edge. She was trying too hard. There was no ease between them. Even though Rachel hadn't seen her sister in over a year and a half, she could still tell when something was amiss, and her sister might as well have been clanging a cymbal over her head.

Rachel shook the thought from her mind and swept her gaze over her sister's slim figure. "You don't even look like you were pregnant. How did you do it?"

"Slowly," Sofia emphasized. "Lyla is almost two years old. You, on the other hand, have had a complete transformation."

"I had little to do in Springdale other than work and exercise."

"It shows, but it's not just that." Sofia cupped Rachel's chin. "It's what I see in your eyes. There is a spark of confidence. Of…peace. I haven't seen those two things in years." Her eyes teared up, and she wiped them away. "I only wish Mom and Dad could see you, too."

Kyle stepped closer. "No. You didn't share anything with them, did you?"

Sofia stepped back. "Of course not. I would never…" Her voice trailed off, and she cleared her throat. Something was definitely off with her. Lyla whimpered, picking up on her mother's subtle distress.

Kyle nodded. "That's good," he said, though he didn't seem satisfied with the answer.

"Do you think it will work?" Sofia asked her sister. "This trap you're setting for Seth?"

"I honestly know little about it," Rachel said. Considering Sofia's strange demeanor, Rachel felt it best to feign ignorance.

Kyle tapped at his watch. "Rachel, I told you we wouldn't have much time."

Lyla walked toward Rachel, and Rachel got down on her knees. She reached out and took the youngster's hands. "I'm so glad I got to see you. You've grown so much."

"I'm big girl."

Rachel smiled through her pain. She had missed so much of her niece's life. In that moment, her body felt heavy with despair. "You're right!" She brought the little girl close, inhaling the scent of her strawberry shampoo and trying to forever stamp it into her memory.

Lyla backed up and rubbed her nose against Rachel's.

Rachel nuzzled her back and then hugged her tight. "Eskimo kisses. Thank you, sweet girl."

Kyle reached under her arm to help her stand up. "I'm sorry, but it's time. This was dangerous as it is. There's a WITSEC inspector ready to take Sofia and Lyla to their safe place. They'll stay with them until this is over. I have people watching your parents as well."

Kyle escorted Sofia and her daughter from the hotel room.

As he walked out, her sister waved. "Please, remember what I said."

It was a message she was leaving. Now Rachel had to decipher it like Seth's notes. Only there wasn't a key to go with it.

SIXTEEN

Kyle watched from his post as Rachel and the agent sat in the vehicle hiding in the woods. He was off in the distance, scoping the scene with a pair of binoculars, hoping that what he expected to happen wouldn't take place, but in his heart knowing it would.

He thought back to the meeting he'd arranged between the sisters. The first hint that something was amiss was the earrings that Sofia had given Rachel and the words she'd spoken to her. *Remember, things are not always what they seem.* It had been a clear warning.

Kyle's intentions behind the meeting had been twofold. Truly, he did want to give Rachel the opportunity to see her sister and niece again. But that wasn't the only reason.

Ever since he'd partnered with Rachel again, he'd wondered if Seth had gotten to Sofia. Kyle had numerous suspicions about the break-in at Sofia's house. The fact that the women had conveniently been gone from the property when the break-in occurred. That the only things taken were Rachel's belongings. His first instinct was that the Black Crew was deep and extensive and was posting 24-7 watch on Rachel's family members. That was certainly possible, but considering the types of people that Seth recruited, was it feasible? Could they keep it up for not just a few days, but weeks to years on end? After the information concerning Dr. Allen came to light, he figured it was more likely that crew members were designated certain duties at certain times.

Kyle knew there was nothing a mother wouldn't do to protect her child. It would be the only way you'd give up your sister—to save your daughter. It wouldn't be done out of spite, but out of necessity.

After their reunion, Kyle reached out to Gage Carter and asked him to look through the plethora of Seth's letters to see if any had been written to Sofia.

A few had been found and decoded. The obtuse language suggested that Seth had his hooks in Rachel's sister.

What Seth's letters suggested in their language to Sofia he hadn't fully disclosed to Rachel, though she was aware that she was in more danger at present than the agent meant to lure Seth from her.

What Kyle did share had broken Rachel's heart.

The earrings Sofia had gifted Rachel had been tracking devices. Both of them. If one got lost, the Black Crew still had the other. The jewelry wasn't a thoughtful birthday gift. They were designed to locate Rachel and bring her to the one person she wanted to see the least.

Seth.

And Kyle was going to let it happen.

The irony of the situation tugged at his heart. Rachel was putting complete trust in him when he wasn't reciprocating. There was an element of need on her part—

her ex-husband wanted her dead, and the DA wanted her charged with murder. DA Elijah Nguyen had been making a celebrity of himself with his on-air musings about Rachel's guilt. Kyle suspected he was a member of the Black Crew but hadn't had the time to prove it. Of course, Rachel had other options that Kyle offered her, but she stuck with his plan.

Didn't that speak more to her innocence? That she had nothing to hide? If she had been working with Seth, then it would be exposed in these next moments. That's another reason why he designed the trap as he had.

It was the ultimate cat-and-mouse game, and if he or Rachel failed on any level, both would die and Seth would fade into the wind. Considering Seth's resources and following, law enforcement wouldn't find him before Seth died of old age. Rachel understood the risks and was willing to take them, because she'd never be free until Seth was behind bars. Then again, would she be free even then? Perhaps her freedom could only come after Seth's demise. If they got him back to prison, they'd have to cut him off from all human contact. No more writing letters. The risk was too great. Unfortunately, even Kyle didn't think he could enforce isolation to such a degree.

If Rachel felt that way as well, would she take matters into her own hands? Would she, if she had the chance, kill Seth? Kyle was used to working through the permutations of a situation, but his stomach sank as he considered that possibility. Rachel had done nothing to disprove her belief in the sanctity of life, but he'd also never put her in the same sphere with someone who took so much of it. Some could argue that killing Seth would prevent death—and a lot of it. In fact, he'd essentially made that argument to her in the hospital when he told her her life was more valuable than his because she could put Seth back behind bars.

Sweat beaded his hairline. If Rachel chose something so dire as to kill Seth, it would be the end of him. Not just of his career, but in all he believed about her. His jaw clenched. If he couldn't live with her doing something so against her character, that meant he was emotionally invested in her. In their relationship.

It meant that he loved her.

And he'd put her in a scenario where she'd likely have to confront her biggest fear. And she trusted him to do that.

Did that mean she loved him as well?

His heart skipped a beat as he pondered the question. Then he quickly chastised himself for having such thoughts out here on a mission. The situation could easily turn deadly if he lost focus. Redirecting his attention, he settled prone on the forest floor and looked through the binoculars again. Rachel was sitting in the vehicle with the WITSEC agent, safe. For now.

That was until Seth came for her.

Rachel knew Kyle hadn't disclosed all the reasons behind the plan or why he'd chosen such drastic measures—using her as bait. It went against everything he believed in. The reason she agreed to it? Because she was willing to risk her own life for freedom.

She bitterly fingered the earrings her sister had given her, now knowing the very thing disguised as a gift had been a signal for her ultimate foe.

What had Seth threatened her sister with? It must have been something to do with Lyla. Would Rachel have done anything differently if she had a child? Could she blame Sofia for wanting to protect Lyla at all costs? Was there anyone she would betray her sister for? Rachel couldn't fathom making the choice, and she certainly would lay her life down for her niece—there was just a middleman in the decision.

Rachel had needed to feel close to her sister in their meeting. Instead, it had been like an appointment with a stranger. The words Sofia had spoken to her kept replaying in her mind. Sofia wasn't the free spirit she'd been in the past.

Kyle had used the arrested cult member Brad Johnson to set a trap for Seth. Through channels, WITSEC had sent Seth a message that Rachel wanted to meet with him at Sofia's residence, to discuss a truce, a way to move forward where they could both be free. They were using a doppelgänger for the meeting—or at least for the initial ruse. Rachel had to admit that from a distance, the woman was indistinguishable from Rachel. Up close was a different story.

All the inspector had to do was get close. Once in Seth's presence, she would arrest him with the help of her surveillance team and get him back in jail to be held until they tried him again. Brad Johnson would confess that Seth had paid him to kidnap Rachel and bring her to him. Rachel shuddered involuntarily at the thought.

If part one of the plan failed—Kyle had instituted part two as the backup, using her as bait. This was the plan most likely to lure out Seth since she wore the earrings.

Rachel hadn't met the WITSEC inspector, Daniel Kruger, who was sitting with her in the car. Young man. Early thirties. Brown eyes. Side-swept longish brown-blond hair. He seemed better suited for a movie screen than law enforcement. He was inexperienced. Not that he confessed it to her, but it was clear in each of his movements. His hands either gripped the steering wheel until his knuckles whitened, or his legs fidgeted so much he'd rock the car. At several points, Rachel had to settle a hand on his thigh to stop the movement. Kruger constantly twirled his thumbs or pressed his index finger into his earpiece, listening closely for any incoming message. He reminded Rachel of a new doctor on their first day as an attending.

Rachel could also listen to the team's communications. Currently, there wasn't any cross chatter. They had been instructed to stay silent except for emergency.

Rachel related to what Kruger was experiencing. The weight of the world could be suffocating. Patients held Rachel to account for the training she acquired and expected her to act proficiently in a crisis. The years of school, internship and fellowship were supposed to enable her to succeed under pressure.

Was there a proving ground for WITSEC inspectors? Could going through a simulation many times be the same as confronting a murderous human? Medical simulation attempted to do the same thing. The benefit was being able to make a mistake without costing a life. It was so different with an actual patient, who reached out with frail hands and watery eyes, imploring for just a few more seconds of time on earth.

Another reason Rachel held so tightly to her faith. There had to be more to this life.

Where was Kyle? He'd said he'd keep a close eye, but she couldn't see him, though admittedly she was trying not to look.

Even though the distance between her and Kyle was palpable, she would have preferred to be sitting with him. Was there a way the two of them could ever be together? Or was it a fantasy that Rachel had latched on to that wasn't possible in the real world?

Could she trust the man she was sitting with?

"What time is the meeting with Seth and Sofia supposed to happen?" Rachel asked.

Daniel consulted his watch. His eyebrows narrowed together, the move clearly giving him time to contemplate how much information he should share with Rachel. People young in their profession clung to the rules. More experienced professionals had ethical boundaries but knew when they could bend the rules—when it was in the interest of the client they were serving.

"I'm sure they have instructed you not to give me a lot of details, but what's it going to hurt if I know the time."

"It's in twenty minutes," Daniel relented with a sigh.

They were in the middle of nowhere. A wooded area shaded by the deciduous trees in full leafy glory. It was a time of year she'd grown to appreciate. How things that once looked dead could bring about new life again. A renewal.

A fresh hope.

The sun was high, though they sat in a shaded area.

Rachel powered down her window, inhaling deeply the scent of earth and wildflowers.

That's when she heard the crunching of tree branches.

Reflexively, she unclipped her seat belt, if for no other reason than to exit the car quickly. Seeing the motion, Daniel reached for her hand. "What are you doing?"

Rachel pressed a finger to her lips and slowly depressed the release button on his seat belt as well. She motioned with a finger to the back of the car. They both turned around.

"There's no one there. You're being hypersensitive," Daniel said unconvincingly.

Paranoia was the red flag of a life that had proven monsters lived under the bed. That's when the perceived loss of mind grew into something more life-preserving—hypervigilance—and Rachel's inner alarm system had been fine-tuned to perfection.

Rachel stared into the woods and slowly examined the trunk of every tree. That's when she saw it—the flash of an arm motioning to another individual. How many people were out there? She took the earrings from her lobes and deposited them in the foot well—their purpose fulfilled.

"They're coming." She pointed. "We need to get out of here."

It was never part of the plan for Rachel to surrender herself. The hope was to get Seth in the same geographic area so WITSEC could apprehend him. Plus, there wasn't any way she could allow herself to suffer any such fate. Rachel was going to fight, and it would not be a ruse.

As they both faced forward, Daniel with his hand on the key to start the engine, two men approached the front of the car. Rachel grabbed Kruger's hand and turned the ignition, reached her leg over his and stomped her foot on the gas. As the car lurched forward, both men jumped out of the way. Daniel took the wheel and steered the car farther down the dirt road.

Gunfire ensued.

It didn't take long before the car couldn't gain traction any longer and lumbered through the dirt and leaves like an elephant stuck in a mud bog. The tires had no doubt been punctured by bullets.

"We've got to bail," Rachel said as she opened her car door, then ran as fast as she could into the woods. She heard Daniel do the same. There was no sense in them trying to stick together. She didn't have any confidence that Kruger could provide protection, and risked it on her own. She slalomed between the trees like a skier fighting for a gold medal on moguls—darting in zigzag patterns between broad trunks to avoid the gunfire. The earth opened underneath her, and she tumbled head over feet into a ditch. After coming to a stop, she scrambled underneath an exposed root ball and stayed still, listening for her pursuers.

They were quiet. She couldn't even hear the faint communication of talking through radios. No voices in her ear of WITSEC agents discussing their plan, which was to fan out through the woods and hunt Seth if the Black Crew showed up. Calling out would disclose her location. How were the Black Crew communicating with one another? Rachel crawled along the length of the ditch. At least she wasn't easily visible from this position. She came to an end and noticed a small river with a few large boulders at its edge. The flow seemed easy enough to traverse, but without knowing the depth, let alone the sound it would make, and the subsequent wet clothes she'd have to deal with, a water escape didn't seem the best idea.

Rachel popped her head up. She could see a man trailing her. She looked upstream and saw a small cottage. It would provide protection but would also be the first place someone would search. It looked well maintained. Would it have a working landline? Cell service in the woods often led people to consider keeping theirs.

Rachel crawled out of the ditch and scrambled to the first boulder by the river. Just as she rounded the back end of it, bullets ricocheted off the top, sending moss-covered rock fragments raining down on her head. She looked at the cottage with renewed interest. Yes, it would be the first place they would look for her, but she could also barricade herself inside, and maybe there'd be a weapon she could use.

Rachel broke into a run and headed for the back side of the cottage. She jiggled the doorknob and found it locked. There was a large window next to the back door. She tested it and found it open. She lifted it and scrambled inside, pulling the window down behind her and latching it. When she turned, she found herself in the kitchen. A phone, harkening back to the '80s, with a long, stretched-out cord, hung on the wall. She yanked off the receiver and listened. No dial tone. She slammed it down. She riffled through the kitchen drawers, looking for something she could defend herself with and strangely found all the deadly knives missing. Nothing better than a butter knife.

That would not help.

Rachel passed through the kitchen door to the front parlor and checked the front latch. It was locked. She tested the windows and quickly pulled the curtains closed. There had to be something here she could use to defend herself.

The fireplace didn't have any utensils beside it. She neared it and was surprised to find the area warm. A few coals glowed red, a faint hiss of steam escaping.

Someone had just been here. Had she just missed someone who could help her? Rachel backtracked toward the kitchen and entered the bedroom. The bed was unmade. She opened the drawer to the bedside table. No gun. She opened the closet doors. No rifles sat inside.

It was almost devoid of anything she could use to defend herself. She looked out the bedroom window and saw a man with a rifle headed her way. She was literally a sitting duck, and the number of men who were trailing her could easily overpower her. She let the curtain fall closed. What could she do? She'd chosen a site that would become her coffin. Seth liked to bury his victims in the woods.

The skin along her spine prickled. The sound of footsteps over creaking, aged floor planks sent electric tingles down her arms and legs, priming her to run, but there wasn't anywhere to go.

Footsteps were an intriguing thing. How easily someone could differentiate the person behind them. Though it had been years since she'd heard them, they were as easily identifiable to her as seeing someone face-to-face.

Because she had hidden from those footsteps for a decade. Feigned sleep when they would come into their bedroom.

She turned around.

"Hi, Rachel. Long time no see, as they say."

Seth had finally found her.

SEVENTEEN

Rachel's heart thrummed wildly at the base of her throat. She covered her neck with her hand. It was hard to swallow. The only sound she would likely make was a high squeak, and she didn't want to be timid in Seth's presence. She was trapped in the room she wanted to be pinned in the least.

Prison had not changed his looks for the worse. His blond-brown hair was longer, stylishly mussed up with hair product. A cleanly shaved face. Seemingly, Seth Black had defied the stress that caused some people to age. The weight he had lost defined his musculature. His look was more refined than she'd thought possible. Put a tux on him and he could be the head of the Boston elite without batting an eye. A wolf in Armani. No one would be the wiser. It wouldn't surprise her in the least if he'd gone keto—driving his body fat to single percentage points. His jaw was angular. His green eyes pierced the very essence of her spirit. What woman wouldn't be attracted to him, to his prestige, to his money?

All of it was a facade. The anger she felt toward herself for not realizing at the beginning that he was a shell of a person hiding a dark, dangerous self still lingered.

"Miss me?" he asked, smiling mischievously. He licked his lips—not seductively, but like an animal who had captured long-hunted prey and was hungry to devour it.

He stepped toward her. She refused to back away and broadened her stance to provide more balance and raised her fists. Seth raised his hands in mock surrender, a childlike mask contorting his face.

"Rachel," he said in a singsong voice, like a mother trying to calm a child from a tantrum. "I would never hurt you. Surely you know that by now. You're the only one I ever protected."

"I don't know you, Seth. I never did. Not your true self. Not until the end."

He took two quick steps toward her and grabbed her wrists. She struggled against his grip, trying to turn her wrists into the weakest part of his hand, where his thumb met his index finger. He clamped harder, and she winced at the pressure.

"Just be still," he seethed. "I'm going to check you for a wire, that's all."

He lifted his hands toward her neck and pulled her hair behind her, glancing into her ears. "Guess you ditched the gift from your sister. They served their purpose well."

Thankfully, he missed the tiny device secured in her ear canal.

"Did you threaten her?" Rachel asked.

"Who?"

"Sofia. Did you tell her you would hurt Lyla?"

He smiled snidely. "I never really liked her, anyway. Too homely."

But that had been the very reason he'd picked Rachel. To blend into the background. To give him the cover of having a normal life.

"A woman who cooperates after you threaten her child isn't an ally," she told him. "She's ultimately an enemy."

"Are you sure? Even after all the money I gave her?"

"What are you talking about?" Rachel asked.

"In your absence, I've been keeping tabs on your sister like, well, any good brother-in-law would do. I'm sure you expected me to do nothing less."

"We're not married anymore. You don't owe my family anything. It strikes me as funny that you suddenly had this desire to be close to them only after you went to prison and I was in hiding."

"Well, that may be what you say, but in my heart I'll always be married to you, regardless of what a piece of paper dictates." He waved his hand in front of his face. "Anyway, your sister and her husband got into a bit of a financial bind. There were some debts they couldn't pay off. My mother was more than happy to float her the money for a little help."

"There's no way she would do that."

"Even if she was going to lose her home? Your precious little niece living on the streets? I couldn't bear thinking about it. Even I'm not that coldhearted."

But he was. He just couldn't fathom the evil within himself. He was so smart, yet so emotionally deficient. Seth didn't possess an empathetic Geiger to register what others were feeling.

Rachel pressed her lips together as she considered his statements. This was additional news if true. Part of the game was figuring out if this was one of those moments of brutal honestly or a torturous lie that would get her to doubt her sister and the loyalty they had to one another. Because of WITSEC, she'd lost the ability to know the ins and outs of her sister's life. What sort of trouble Sofia was in.

Seth dug his fingers into Rachel's shoulders and yanked her forward, unbuttoning the top of her shirt and running his fingers across her neckline. Not gently, like a man who loved her would do. Instead he pressed hard enough to make her flinch. He lifted the bottom of her shirt and exposed her belly. Embraced her in an uncomfortable hug and pressed her against him as he patted down her back.

Her stomach roiled. A cold sweat broke out at the base of her neck. He stepped back and ran his hands down her legs. He pushed her to sit on the bed and took off her shoes and socks, reaching up into her loose pants and leaving a slick trail of fear in the wake of his touch. These moves were to both check for a wire and hinder her ability to escape. Running in bare feet across sticks and rocks would slow her down no matter how much adrenaline numbed her nerve endings.

He knelt before her and placed his hands on her lower back and pulled her forward. "I only ever loved you, Rachel. My release from prison—don't you see God's hand in it?"

Another difference between them had been their disparate beliefs in God. He'd often laughed at her faith. Called her weak for putting trust in something that couldn't be seen, felt or heard. Now he was using it to build a bridge back to her. But after having experienced life out from under Seth's shadow, she'd rather be homeless than seek comfort built on a shaky house of cards.

"No, I don't. I see that somehow you manipulated the courts or, at the very least, one juror to rig the system to set you free."

He ignored her taunt. Instead, he eased back and stood up, taking two steps back. He placed his hands on his hips, holding her in his gaze for an uncomfortable length of time. Simply another tactic to exert his power over her. "You look amazing."

The sound of a tree branch breaking drew his attention to the window, and he took two steps toward it to look out. As soon as the exit to the bedroom door was clear, she ran through it. Seth quickly shifted his direction, and in three steps, kicked her feet out from underneath her, sending her face-first into the wood floor. She cracked her chin, blood spurting forth immediately. Lights starred her vision. She rested her cheek against the floor, resisting the lure to close her eyes.

That would be the peaceful path. Surrendering into the darkness. Letting him have his way with her. Wasn't this always going to be the inevitable end?

Then she heard it. A voice in her ear. Kyle.

"Rachel, I'm here. I see you. I'm with you. Get back up. You're okay."

Seth decided her next move for her and grabbed the waistband of her jeans, hoisting her up. "Rachel, Rachel. There's no need to be so dramatic." She tried to look at his face through her blurred vision. "Now, look at what you've done. Marked up that new, shiny face of yours."

He pulled her into the kitchen and plopped her into a chair. Blood dripped onto her shirt, and she used the back of her hand to put pressure on the gash. Seth stepped to the sink and washed his hands, once again the surgeon prepping for the OR.

Stepping in front of her, he placed his thumb and forefinger on her jaw—pressing in, viselike. Rachel whimpered and knocked his hand away. Without hesitation, he backhanded her across the face, knocking her from the chair.

Her vision blackened.

Kyle's voice crackled in her ear. "Rachel… Rachel…"

Rachel had to move to a sitting position, or he'd storm in. Getting knocked down twice would be hard for Kyle to stand. She had to get back into the game. They didn't have enough information from Seth to lock him away forever. She had to get more.

Her vision was fuzzy. She could see Seth's figure at the window peering out. Rachel pushed up onto all fours, the world spinning, and set her feet to the ground to stand. Grabbing a musty seat cushion from one of the other kitchen chairs, folding and holding it to her body, she rested her head on it. It was funny how one insignificant item seemed to provide enough of a barrier between her and Seth to feel like she had some space to breathe and think. She sat back in the chair.

"You're making me act like a terrible man, Rachel."

In all their years of marriage, he hadn't been violent with her. Now, the gloves were off. Maybe it was the change in her demeanor, her physicality, that told him she wasn't willing to submit to his intimidation anymore.

So he had to prove that he still had power over her.

Her heart ached. She hated the position she was in. She missed Kyle—physically ached for his closeness. Every time Seth touched her, he caused pain. For Seth, Rachel's needs were never considered. Kyle was the opposite. He'd always put her first. She didn't desire to ever be with a man like Seth again.

It was better to be alone if she couldn't be with Kyle.

"I'm here, Rachel. I've got you. You're not alone," Kyle said into her ear.

She wept into the cushion. His words provided strength. There was a panic button placed behind one knee, another item Seth had missed, that she could press if she felt out of control. An exit if she couldn't take what Seth brought on. There was also a word she could say. But they needed more from Seth. More of a confession to put him behind bars for good.

She felt her chin. The wound was open, and it would need stitches. She stretched her neck—it was sore from the impact of the slap and subsequent fall, but nothing a few ibuprofens and a heating pad wouldn't fix.

Seth got down on one knee and took her hands in his. "I want you, Rachel. I want you to come away with me."

Cool saliva flooded her mouth. She clenched her teeth to keep from vomiting. She didn't know if the feeling was just from his words or the cumulative effects of her recent injury, portending a concussion.

She wiggled her hands free from his and pulled the pillow closer to her body.

"I can make you," he said.

Rachel thought through trying to reason with him. It was always tit for tat. She'd never get ahead, but she also had a job to do. She had to help herself secure her freedom.

"How?" Rachel asked.

"You know about the woman found in the woods with your hair on her body."

"Is that what you really want? To see me go to jail for a crime I didn't commit?"

He pulled a chair from the table and sat down. "If I had known you could be this way, feisty and assertive, I would have never become the man that I was."

Psychopaths always resorted to this—blaming the victim for their own deficits. It pulled her back into his sick emotional web. She would not do it. Three years of being free from it had given her the clarity she needed.

"You're claiming my weight and timidity caused you to be a serial killer?"

"I just needed…more excitement. I hear from the Black Crew that you're quite the fiery one. Like to fight back. Throw a few punches."

Rachel couldn't travel down this road with him. It was a highway too far into the abyss. She wasn't going to cross this line to entertain his morbid fantasies.

"Where is Dr. Allen?" she asked.

"Closer than you think."

Rachel raised an eyebrow. Had Kyle heard that?

"You're using her?"

Seth shrugged. "I may love her, too."

Love to Seth was nothing more than a bargaining chip. Something he used as a weapon to get women to yield to his ways. She could never imagine Kyle using anyone, let alone someone he claimed to love, just to hurt them. In fact, it pained Kyle to feel love for someone that he couldn't give himself fully to.

"What is it you have that makes you think I would go with you?"

"Evidence," he said simply.

"What kind?"

"Signed documents from Dr. Allen from your sessions that you colluded in my crimes. That we were partners." His green eyes sparkled with pride. "I understand you were fascinated with my work."

How did he know about her murder boards? Someone in the Black Crew must have told him. She closed her eyes and pressed into the conversation. This could be the thing law enforcement needed to make sure Seth never got past the razor-wire fence. Perhaps they'd finally relegate him to the supermax facility in Colorado where he'd only see the outside for an hour a day.

"How many did I have right?" Rachel challenged.

He leaned toward her, taking her hand in his. He wedged his fingers between hers and squeezed, not releasing the pressure.

"Most were correct. A few were outliers, but you discovered some that even law enforcement hadn't found."

Rachel clenched her teeth to keep from crying at the pain in her hands. "What were their names? How long did you torture them?"

Seth rattled off the names of five women like a birthday wish list.

Rachel's heart rammed into her ribs. She found it hard to take a deep breath. How could she get out of this? They had enough now. He'd admitted to murders that they hadn't yet found him guilty of.

The evidence against Dr. Allen was mounting, too, but would it be enough for people to believe that she'd done things under Seth's influence? Rachel wanted more against Dr. Allen. It was as if Seth was trying to protect her...or maybe just trying to protect the position that she held with WITSEC. If she worked where she did, Seth had a mole at a high level he could depend on.

"They know about the letters," Rachel said. "That you and Dr. Allen were—"

"Exchanging letters isn't a crime. If you had them fully deciphered, you'd realize that there isn't much there."

Rachel bit her lip. He could be right. She didn't fully know what all the documents contained.

"If you come with me," Seth said, "I'll have Nora destroy the evidence. You'll be free."

"All except for my hair that was recently found on one of your victims. How are you going to explain that away?"

He clicked his tongue against the roof of his mouth. "Yeah, that. We might have to put our heads together on that one. Nothing that two smart people can't come up with a solution to. Does that mean you're in? You'll come with me?" He pulled her into an awkward embrace. "I love you, Rachel. We can start over. We'll go overseas. Europe or something. I won't want the other women if you give me what I need."

Women who were caregivers were at high risk of becoming involved in codependent relationships. It was the first time it was crystal clear in her mind. Maybe this thought had always played in her subconscious. Maybe deep down she'd always known what Seth was and had an inherent desire to fix him. She was a doctor, a smart one, and it shouldn't be beyond her capabilities to do so.

This was the lie she survived on—subconsciously or not. But Seth was the only one who could choose to do the work to fix himself. And he'd never see it. Whether it was nature, or nurture, or an evil seed—it didn't matter. He'd have to strike the match himself, and it was something he'd never be capable of doing.

But right now, Rachel had to get him to believe she was back in this game with him, and she didn't know how good an actress she was.

Rachel tensed the muscles in her arm to keep her hand from trembling as she reached out and settled her palm against his face.

"I'll go with you," Rachel said. "You don't know how long I've waited for you to say those words to me. Three years was too long to be apart. But if you want me to go with you, tell me the truth about Nora. There will not be another woman coming between us. I must be your one and only."

It was every codependent dream come true. That they had fully encased the partner in the web.

"I'll tell you everything. I don't love her. There's no way I could. She's no match for you. She killed Penelope and put your hair there to frame you for it."

And he pressed his lips against hers.

Kyle was desperate to reach Rachel. The sound of her smacking the floor when Seth tripped her had been one thing. The slap across her face had split his heart in two and simultaneously fueled his blood with anger.

Now it was time to end this interaction. She'd done it.

Gotten him to confess enough incriminating evidence to put him away for a lifetime. Cleared herself from the murder they accused her of. They had enough to put Nora Allen behind bars for good, too.

He was constantly scanning the woods for members of the Black Crew. What surprised him was how few there were. As soon as Rachel had gone into the house, WITSEC agents had flooded into the woods to capture those that had approached the car, and all had been secured. Inspector Kruger was now working with Kyle, though he couldn't be seen. They were in radio contact, approaching the cottage from different angles.

"Daniel. Check in."

No response. Had they missed someone? They had accounted for the men who had approached the car. Had Seth hidden Black Crew members farther out? Anything was possible in this situation.

He heard running footfalls behind him. He turned on his belly in that direction, drawing his weapon from his holster, and couldn't fathom what he was seeing. A woman in a business suit, running in heels straight at him, holding a baseball bat above her head.

"Dr. Allen! Drop the bat or I'll shoot."

She didn't listen and began screaming at the top of her lungs. He fired a shot, missed and then raised his hand as she aimed the bat at his head. He blocked the first swing, heard a crack of bone. As he dropped his defensive arm, she clocked him again to the side of the head.

All went black.

EIGHTEEN

"Kyle…"

His name whispered in the distance. The sound of rushing blood in his ears nearly drowning it out. His head pounded, and he felt cold and sweaty. His body felt heavy. Pulling his hands forward, he tried to assess the damage, but found they were bound behind his back.

A foot nudged his knee. The movement made his head pound more.

"Kyle…wake up."

Rachel's voice. Low but insistent. He blinked a few times. Then he turned toward the direction of her voice and opened his eyes. They were sitting side by side in a kitchen, zip-tied to rickety wooden chairs. His vision turned red, and he blinked a few more times to see blood dripping onto his lap. He couldn't remember another situation with a witness where he'd gotten so many injuries—and the crisis wasn't over yet.

He swished saliva around his mouth, his body begging for a drink of water. "Where are they?"

"In the bedroom," Rachel said. "Is anyone else coming?"

Kyle shook his head. "I don't know. On the radio, I couldn't raise Daniel. I don't know where anyone is right now. We... I might have underestimated the number of people Seth had hiding out." He turned to look at her. Her chin was bruised, the laceration open and still oozing blood. Nothing that couldn't be fixed—at least physically. But what he'd asked her to do, and she'd volunteered for—would there be any fixing that? In the woods, praying with everything in him for Rachel's protection, he'd realized one thing.

He loved her.

There was no denying it. She was everything to him. Every injury to her body he could feel on his own, and it tore him to pieces that his actions had caused her to suffer. He had to stop this—stop Seth.

Stop him forever.

And somehow, he had to convince Rachel that he'd been wrong on every level. That she was the one for him. He'd figure out a way for them to be together.

If she would have him.

He held her eyes. "I'm sorry."

"Kyle, it's okay. I knew what I was getting into."

"Can you break free?" he asked.

Rachel wiggled at her bindings and then shook her head.

Kyle did the same, finding them loose enough to break his hands free.

At that moment, Seth and Nora stepped into the kitchen. Kyle kept his hands clasped behind his back. The only explanation for the loose bindings was that perhaps Nora had been the one to tie him up. Seth's fascination with the new Rachel had perhaps made her the biggest prize—the one most worthy of his attention.

"Looks like our sleeping beauty has awakened," Seth said. He stayed out of arm's reach.

"What's your plan, Seth?" Kyle asked.

"For you, it's easy. Looks like your time on earth will end soon."

"That much I gathered."

"What about Nora?" Rachel challenged. "I thought you told me you were done with her."

Rachel was providing the ultimate distraction.

Nora snapped her head toward Seth. "What is she talking about?" she demanded. "You said killing the two of them was the only way to end this situation so we could have the life we've been planning for years."

Kyle eased his arm forward. His holster was empty. That's when he saw his weapon in Seth's hand.

Hopefully, he was a bad shot.

Kyle bolted from his chair and charged Seth. It didn't take Seth more than a second to raise his arm, take aim, and fire off a shot. Searing fire bloomed in Kyle's chest, and the force knocked him backward onto the ancient wood floor. Darkness filled his vision again.

"Kyle!"

Rachel's was not a scream to rouse him, but a cry of desperation, hoping he was still alive. And that's when she knew her feelings had crossed over. It was the sound she heard in the ER only under the direst circumstances. A wail. And now it made sense to her that prayer could happen when words could not be spoken.

When words couldn't be formed because the well of darkness was too deep.

No... No... No... Her thoughts screamed inside her head.

Be calm... She heard another voice break through.

She inhaled sharply and watched for the rise and fall of his chest. Only a momentary reprieve when she saw his ribs heave.

Rachel looked directly at Seth and tried to affect the look of contrition. The words she said next had to be believable. "Seth, you need to untie me right now. Let me help Inspector Reid. If he dies, you and I will always be hunted. We could never be together."

It was a gamble. She was hoping the statements he'd made to her were truthful—one of the few times he'd spoken authentically—or at least what Seth believed to be honesty. Seth walked toward her and clipped the zip ties from her wrists.

Rachel dropped to her knees. She placed her ear above Kyle's mouth and nose while simultaneously slipping two fingers into the crease of his neck. He was breathing. His pulse was quick but relatively strong. She tore his shirt open, buttons flying off into the distance. The bullet had entered the left chest, just above his Kevlar vest, near the shoulder joint. Taking off the vest, she placed a knuckle on his sternum and rubbed hard. It wasn't the kindest thing to do, but she needed him to wake up. Needed him with her.

He inhaled sharply and shoved her hand away. It was the exact response she was looking for. He pushed up to a sitting position, blinking rapidly, and took several deep inhalations, his eyes cringing as he did so. Rachel reached up to the kitchen table and grabbed a towel and put pressure on the wound. It could be a good sign it wasn't bleeding much. It could also mean he was losing a lot of blood internally, hidden from her eyes. If that was happening, it was only a matter of time before shock set in. Just like when he had taken a bullet to the gut.

Kyle met Rachel's eyes with a weary smile, but a spark of light was present in his demeanor. Her heart rate settled a bit.

Kyle reached for his phone in his back pocket and realized it was missing. "Dr. Allen, I suggest you give me my phone. I have something to play for you. It might change your mind about linking your life with Seth's in whatever plans you have made."

He could speak full sentences. Another sign that his lung and large blood vessels were okay. However, he wasn't able to move his left arm much, the bullet likely destroying the joint to the point he would require surgery.

Nora Allen noticed the phone on the table, and both she and Seth reached for it at the same time. She gripped it in both hands and walked slowly to Kyle.

Seth trained his weapon again on Kyle and fired off a shot. Kyle clenched his eyes closed. The gun jammed, and Seth threw it aside in disgust. Kyle exhaled slowly. Without the vest in place, that shot would have proved fatal.

"Nora," Seth pleaded. "This isn't a good idea. He's going to try and turn you against me. I've pledged my love to you. This whole thing was for *you*. So we could be together. The idea was to end these two and go on with life as we wanted it. Don't you remember? All those letters where I said those very things for years?"

Kyle raised his right hand and beckoned Dr. Allen to him. "If you want to know the truth, Nora, you're going to want me to play the things he said to Rachel while you were outside. I think they'll be very enlightening."

Nora hesitated, her eyes darting across the room as she tried to make a decision.

Kyle continued. "Right now, all this is fixable. You have hurt no one. The things you've done…are forgivable, but before you cross that line, you need to understand that what this man has convinced you to be true is a lie."

She squared her shoulders and handed Kyle his phone. He balanced the device on his knee, using the face ID to get inside, and scrolled through a series of voice recordings.

"Nora, you know what the government is capable of. This recording is a fake," Seth said. "This is engineered by WITSEC so you won't believe me anymore. The only reason this man and Rachel are still alive is because the gun jammed."

"Does it surprise you?" Kyle asked the psychologist.

"What?" Nora responded.

"That Rachel is still alive. If he intended to do what he said, why not kill her right away? Why keep her around? It would have been better to make quick work of both of us and be on your way—to the life he promised you."

Nora turned back to Seth. "Yes, why is she still here?"

"She's only been here a short time. We had things to…settle."

Kyle didn't stop. He forged ahead with his argument. "Notice there're no weapons here. He used my gun against me. Where are the knives? How was he going to kill her?"

A cloudy veil dropped over Nora's face. Kyle's words were having an effect. Doubt had slipped into her mind.

Kyle hit Play, and the conversation that Rachel and Seth had within the last hour filled the cabin. Seth moved toward Kyle, but Nora stayed him with a motion of her hand. As soon as she heard Seth's declaration of love, Nora's face reddened. She paced to where Seth had discarded the gun to and picked it up.

And pointed it at Seth.

"You lied! How could you do this to me?" Nora seethed. "I gave up *everything* for you. My life. My home. You said you loved me."

A smirk spread over Seth's face, his true nature revealed through the facade. What did he care about what Nora thought now? He had done what he most wanted to do. If what Seth had said to Rachel was true, then the relationship Seth had developed with Nora had only been to lure Rachel back to him. Nora Allen had simply been collateral damage.

And Seth knew it.

And now he was going to relish letting Nora know she meant nothing to him.

A weight of darkness fell onto Rachel, and her skin pricked at its presence. She hadn't felt it in years—not until this moment when Seth let his mask drop and was going to let Nora see the man he really was.

The monster within was going to expose himself.

"How could you be so stupid? You, with your PhD

in psychology, and you believed the words of a psychopath over your own training."

Allen was apoplectic. The realization contorted her features. "I'll never get it back." She waved the gun Kyle's direction. "What he says is only partly true. If I stop here, I may not go to jail, but my career is over. The first thing the Bureau of Prisons will do is fire me. The licensing board will yank my credentials. My life…is over."

The last words were whispered in disbelief.

Seth stepped toward her. "You have no one to blame but yourself. You're a pitiful human being. You don't deserve me. My mind. My followers."

Tears ran down her face. Her shoulders dropped, shame overcoming her like a weighted blanket. There was no comfort she could find.

"Nora, it's not you. It's him," Rachel said. "Yes, you made some mistakes. So did I. Your life can go on. You need to join me in getting him convicted. Your life won't be the same, but regardless of what happens, it will be better when you're free from him."

Nora squared her shoulders. Rachel's heart quickened. The look said she had resigned herself to a course of action that she couldn't be swayed from. A resolve had cemented itself in her mind. The only thing Rachel couldn't calculate was what it meant for the rest of them.

"She's right," Nora said, turning toward Seth. "I need to be free from you. All women need to be free from you."

She raised the gun and fired the weapon. This time a bullet discharged and hit Seth square in the belly. He fell, holding his gut, blood sluicing through his fingers.

And then Nora Allen ran through the door into the woods.

"I've got him," Kyle said. "You're the only one who can go get her."

Rachel stood on her bare feet and took off running.

NINETEEN

Rachel was a good two hundred yards behind Nora when she broke free from the cabin. She glanced from side to side, looking for additional foes, and didn't see any members of the Black Crew trying to annihilate her.

Rocks and sticks punctured into her feet like Legos strewn by a petulant child. She focused her vision on Allen's back. She was gaining on her. The woman's choice of footwear was hindering her. Not spiked heels, but close. Nora had tripped several times, even stopped momentarily, perhaps with thoughts of removing them, turning once in Rachel's direction to fire off a shot before she thought better of it.

Rachel pumped her arms faster. Her legs followed suit. She found herself gaining on Nora, only ten to fifteen steps behind. She picked up her pace and reached her arm out, brushing the back of Nora's worsted wool jacket. The movement dropped her back a few paces. She roared forward, launched herself into the air, and when she came down, she grabbed one of Allen's feet and hung on long enough to trip her.

Allen tumbled, leaves and sticks scratching her face

and body. The fall knocked the gun from her hand, and it rolled out of reach. Nora screamed as Rachel scurried and tackled her from behind just as she had gotten up on all fours to take off again. Rachel pulled Nora's arms behind her back and held them tight.

"Rachel, please let me go. I won't ever do anything to you. You know my life is over if the police get hold of me."

Rachel's heart broke for her. Was this manipulation or an honest sentiment? Either could be true. Allen could be closer to Seth's demeanor than Rachel wanted to admit.

"Seth will never let you go," Rachel said.

"Seems like he already did, in favor of you," she grunted between breaths.

Rachel shifted her weight off Allen's back and knelt next to her, continuing to grasp her hands.

"I'm sorry you got tangled in Seth's web."

"I did it by choice, and so did you."

Rachel's mouth dropped. "Hardly—"

"I'm so tired of women claiming to be innocent when they know full well what is happening. You can't tell me that in the years you were with Seth, you did not know what he was up to."

"I didn't."

"But you did. You just didn't want to admit it to yourself."

That dug deep into Rachel's chest. It was the one thing about herself that she dreaded was true. That all along, she'd known the truth somewhere in her subconscious but had pushed it down, through disbelief, through denial, and crafted for herself an alternate reality. When her husband wasn't abusive, he was loving and kind. Those moments were survival respites. She'd been deluded to think that his obsessiveness about her whereabouts, about her dress, were signs he loved her more than anything, when all he was doing was trying to possess her as a cover story. Surely, a woman who had spent so many years with him and went back to him knew to her very core that he wasn't innocent.

"What you say about me might be true—probably is true. That I should have known. That I could have done more if I had just been clear in my thinking and analyzed the situation. But you know what he is, and you want to be with him. You planted evidence on one of his victims to implicate me in crimes that I was never a part of. I might have been foolish. Misled. Eager to hope that my husband wasn't the monster that he is. But you? You're just evil."

One of Nora's hands slipped from Rachel's grip. She rolled away from Rachel, pulled a knife from a sheath at her ankle that had been covered by her slacks and rolled back toward Rachel.

Rachel put her hand up in a defensive move, but the knife plunged through her hand and into her belly. Nora scurried to her feet.

"Seth loves me. And now that you'll be out of the picture, we can move forward with framing you for his crimes. He'll be free and we'll be together."

Rachel blinked as Nora backed away from her and then turned to walk off nonchalantly, as if she had not a care in the world.

Rachel fell back onto her haunches and looked down at her current situation. It wasn't good. It was true— the flood of adrenaline into her system was an amazing painkiller, for a few moments, at least, until her brain registered what had occurred and her abdomen seared with pain. She fell onto her back and pressed her free hand over the impaled one, shoving it against her belly to prevent too much blood loss.

The pain halted her breathing. She clenched her eyes and prayed. Who would find her? Seth was injured. The location of the other agents in the woods was unknown. Probably they were tied up arresting all the members of the Black Crew that surrounded the cabin.

A groan escaped her lips. She didn't want to die this way. She had never wanted to die at Seth's hands—or by an agent directed by him. It was the ultimate folly. She'd done so much to be set free, and now she would be buried because, in her delusion, she'd thought she'd freed herself. In reality, she'd just gone back to ultimately be killed by her great foe.

Her thoughts drifted to Kyle. She yearned for him to find her but in the same breath dreaded his arrival. He would blame himself for her injuries, even though she had agreed to risk her life as part of the plan. As part of fully reclaiming the woman she had transitioned to in the desert. That was important if they were going to have a relationship.

Blood flooded through her fingertips. She felt it dripping down her sides and pooling behind her back. The wound was close to her left upper side—where her spleen was located. She would bleed out quickly if the organ was injured. She was too far away to get medical help in time if that was the case. She looked at the sky. It was blue, calm. She felt peaceful.

But she didn't want to surrender to it.

Lord, I know You're the author and perfector of life.
That each breath and heartbeat is granted at Your plea-
sure. Please, spare my life. Give me more time to right
the wrongs of my past. My death will become Kyle's
burden, and I don't want the man I love to feel guilty
over a death he had no control over.

A determination rose within her. Seth could not,
would not, have the last word on her life. She wasn't
meant to die this way. Her work wasn't done. There was
one person she loved, and she would not give that up
without a fight. Rachel crossed her legs, one over the
other, pressing the panic button planted behind her knee.

She spoke—hopefully loud enough for the earpiece
to pick up. "Kyle... I'm hurt... I need you."

Turning her head to the side, she scanned the ground
for the gun Nora had left behind. In order to help Kyle
find her in time, she had to signal him by firing a shot
into the air. With her free hand, she brushed over the
forest undergrowth, her fingers inching through dense
ground cover. Nothing. Now she had to turn her body
the other way to search the other side. Through tears
and static breaths, she pivoted, searching the ground
for the gun.

Each time she tried to take a deep breath to scream,
the pain exploded white-hot through every nerve. Now,
each movement was causing the same thing to happen.
Whimpering, she made one last attempt and dug her
fingers into the dirt, clawing as far out as she could.

Her fingertips touched something metallic and warm.

Kyle heard the words come across his earpiece. Daniel Kruger was with him, putting handcuffs on Seth

Black. A team of paramedics who worked with WIT-SEC in situations like this had made their way to the cottage. Kyle stood and headed to the front door of the cottage. He'd seen the direction that Rachel had darted off in and got a bearing on the tree line.

"Inspector Reid, you can't go after her. You're injured," Daniel said.

Ignoring Daniel, Kyle motioned for the paramedics to follow him. He drew his weapon and raced into the woods. His left arm was in a sling, hindering his running, but nothing was going to stop him from finding Rachel. He had to. He wasn't going to let this happen again. This time it was more than losing a witness.

It was losing someone he loved and couldn't live without.

He ran faster. There were signs someone had gone this way. A trail of stomped grass. Newly broken twigs. He climbed over a few fallen logs.

"Rachel, I'm coming! Stay with me. Call out. I need to hear your voice so that I can find you."

He stopped to listen for the sound of her voice. Hearing nothing, he continued to run, trying to fine-tune his hearing for any vocalization she might make. If she was injured too badly, her voice would not be strong enough to be heard.

Lord, please. I know I'm horrible at this whole prayer thing, but I need You to keep her alive. Rachel needs You. Help me find her. Guide my steps in the right direction.

A gunshot broke through the silence of the woods. A flock of birds scattered into the air to his right. It was Rachel. It had to be.

And if it wasn't, he was willing to risk it.

"This way!" He motioned to the medics.

They followed without question, and Kyle couldn't help but feel astonished by their actions. He knew their edict—they could only help a patient when the scene was safe and there wasn't any question they were heading into unknown danger. Even though Kyle felt assured that it was Rachel trying to signal for help, they didn't, and it would have been within their rights to stop and wait.

Finally, he saw Rachel lying in the distance, perhaps one hundred yards away. Sharp pains zinged through his chest, but he ran harder. If the worst outcome happened, he would not let her die alone.

Kyle pulled up to a stop when he found her, and his breath left him, as if he'd fallen straight onto his back from a high roof. She was on her back, her left hand pinned to her abdomen, a knife thrust through it.

She was pale. The gun lay at her right side, her hand covering it but not gripping it. He walked the last two steps and knelt next to her, reaching underneath her head to cradle it with his good arm.

"You found me." Her words were a whisper. She was breathing rapidly, her face contorted in pain.

"Of course I did. There are two medics with me… I need you to stay with me so they can help you." The pair, a man and a woman, reached them then and opened their trauma packs. One grabbed an oxygen mask and began connecting the end to a tank. He could hear the hiss as the man turned it on. The female EMT grabbed a package of gauze and started stringing together some IV fluids.

The woman grabbed her radio. "I need the cooler

from our rig to our location ASAP. I mean, run it here."
A pair of trauma shears flashed, and they cut the bottom of Rachel's shirt open to the hand that was impaled.

"Kyle…"

His heart knew what was happening, and he shook his head and leaned it next to hers. He couldn't bear to witness the look in her eyes. He'd been in too many of these situations not to know what that look meant. The overwhelming desire to utter those last words when a person didn't think they were going to make it. Once those words were uttered, death soon followed, the spirit considering the work complete and moving on to other realms.

"No—" Kyle moaned. "Stay with me."

"Thank you." The words split him in half. What did she really have to thank him for? For allowing her to put herself in this situation? For him not protecting her? For not keeping her from Seth Black's evil ways? From the Black Crew?

"I'm free…it's okay," Rachel said. "Get him…jail. You have enough."

But he needed her. Not just to testify. He needed her always.

Kyle rested her head onto the ground and reached for her free hand, squeezing it hard. Sobs racked his body, and he pressed his head into the side of her chest and pleaded. "Rachel, stay with me. You can't leave me. Not like this." In his mind, if he gripped her hand hard enough, he could anchor her to the earth. Keep her from leaving.

Keep her from leaving him.

Her eyes closed—but there was one more phrase.

"I love you."

TWENTY

Kyle stood outside Rachel's hospital room. She was back at the hospital where her career started, except on the other side of the experience. She was alive... stable, but not yet ready to wake up. Her eyes would briefly flirt with opening and quickly close. Her hand was repaired and bandaged. A central line snaked into her chest. The nurse discontinued the last bag of blood that hung on the IV pole. He'd lost count of how many bags there had been.

She was in a tenuous position. Her injuries were extensive. The knife had sliced through several sections of bowel and lacerated her spleen; the only way they could save her life was to take it out. Her medical team credited the paramedics with saving her life. They'd had four pints of O-negative blood on their rig—enough to replace the lost volume to keep her clinging to life and get her to the OR. Her blood counts were finally stabilizing.

Rachel looked completely washed out. The color of her face was indistinguishable from the starched pillow it rested upon. Word had spread throughout the hospital of her presence. A HIPAA violation for sure, but there was little that could stop the furtive whispers of hospital gossip when one of their own was within their walls. Particularly one who'd been married to the infamous Seth Black and had been accused of murder herself.

The ER team and surgical staff had evaluated Kyle's injury. Surgery to his left shoulder was necessary, but he'd been putting the doctors off until he felt Rachel was out of the woods. That time hadn't come yet. He'd made so many mistakes and wasn't going to leave her side until he could rest assured she'd live.

A man approached. Kyle assumed he was a member of Rachel's medical team. The semblance of a suit filled his peripheral vision. When he turned, it was Inspector Armijo.

Kyle faced him. "You're the last person I'd thought I'd see."

"How is she?" Javier asked.

Kyle turned back to the window. "Stable, but she hasn't really woken up yet. Her eyelids will flutter, but that's about it. They had to remove her spleen and part of her bowel. Several tendons in her hand needed repair."

"She's alive. She'll work her way back—of this I have no doubt. I heard they found Dr. Allen. Once Seth is out of the hospital, he'll be back in jail. Those are all wins."

Kyle swallowed hard. Yes, they were. On the law enforcement side. But was it a win in the personal sense? Was it ultimately a win that mattered? To those women who wouldn't fall victim to Seth, of course it was. But was there any stopping Seth's particular brand of evil? Could his metastatic reach ever be stopped? Could they restrict his rights to where he wouldn't ever be able to communicate with a person again?

"It was risky, what you did," Javier said.

"I know. She begged me. I didn't feel like anyone else in the agency believed me as far as her innocence. I couldn't trust anybody. I made a judgment call. A bad one, maybe. Probably."

Armijo shoved his hands in his pocket, turned and leaned against the window so he was face-to-face with Kyle.

"I was one of them who didn't believe you or her, but those tapes are convincing. Yes, it was risky. I don't think WITSEC will forgive you for the judgment call. If they do, I'm not sure what kind of job you'll have. Fieldwork may be out of the question."

"It's okay. I don't expect WITSEC to ever take me back, to be honest."

The man nodded. "Looks like we're both out of a job...for the same reasons."

"The same?" Kyle questioned. "I didn't betray a witness."

"Didn't you, though? You chose to put her in harm's way...because you loved her. You knew the only way you could save her was to clear her name. And the only way to do that was to risk her life."

Kyle looked at Rachel's sleeping form. Javier was right. They had acted for the same basic reason, even though Javier had twisted his version to a story he could tell himself that exonerated him from some truly abhorrent actions. As Rachel had said to him on many occasions, denial was the most powerful human defense mechanism.

"Don't you think it's time you tell her how you really feel?" Javier asked.

Kyle pressed his lips together.

"Once you find the woman you can't live without, do everything in your power to keep her with you. Even if it means losing everything." He laid a hand on Kyle's shoulder. "Sometimes, the very things we think we can't live without are those things we should lose in order to have the life that was meant for us."

Rachel shifted. Her last memory was of the woods. The knife. All the blood. Kyle...begging her to stay with him. She'd wanted to, for a moment, but some injuries were too devastating for a person no matter their will to live.

She opened her eyes to a dark room. Shapes were blurry. The soft beeping of a monitor tickled her ears, the sound quickening as she focused on it—it was her heartbeat. She was alive. Still on earth. Her mouth was dry, sticky. Her lips chapped. She pulled her shoulders down. Her left hand ached as she lifted it. It was heavily bandaged, with small drops of dried blood on the outside of the Kerlix gauze. Her other hand was free, and she felt her abdomen. A large dressing was present, and she wondered how many organs she still had left. Enough to ensure her survival? There was a tug at her neck as she looked out the window. She reached for it. A central line. Looking up, she saw the bag of IV fluids hanging. There'd be no need for a central line unless she'd been a critical patient. Likely for blood. How many pints? She wasn't sure she wanted to know.

When she rested her hand back down, it landed on a head of hair.

It was as if a bolt of electricity plowed through Kyle's body. He sat up ramrod straight and looked at her. A look of utter relief washed over his face. He grabbed her uninjured hand and pressed it against his lips, kissing it softly.

She felt a warm tenderness spread through her body. A sense of peace washed over her.

"I'm so glad I get to see your blue eyes again," he whispered softly. "You're beautiful."

She tried to laugh, but the slight movement of her abdominal muscles sent waves of pain through her midsection.

Kyle caressed her arm with his hand. "Shh…that wasn't meant to be funny."

Rachel inhaled. Kyle rustled through her covers and handed her a button. "Here." He pressed it into her palm. "The nurse said when you woke up to give you this. To press it if you're hurting."

That said a lot. The medical team had expected her to wake up. That was a good sign.

"Seth's in jail. Nora, too. He's never getting out again. They found more evidence in Nora's home that she framed you for Penelope Schmidt's murder. That she and Seth were…having an affair, I guess is the safest way to say it." He paused a second, then said, "There's one more thing I need to tell you."

Rachel shifted, trying to find a comfortable spot. "What is it?"

"In hopes of securing a deal with the prosecutor,

Nora disclosed what happened to Dr. Lewis—Seth's previous partner."

"Let me guess, he's not alive anymore."

"No." Kyle smoothed his hand over her lower leg. "At least his family will have closure. Nora will replace him in providing testimony against Seth."

"I don't care about the two of them anymore. I only care about the life I have left and what that looks like."

What would become of her? WITSEC was optional, but she didn't know if she could endure that prison again. Not alone. She'd rather risk the threat from the Black Crew and go back to her old life—or what remained of it—and live with the risk if she could be with those she loved. The loneliness of the last three years had been too much.

"I can't go back."

"Rachel, you'll be killed if you don't. The Black Crew—we might be able to stop them if we hide you, but if we don't, there will be no protecting you. I can't let that happen. I won't let it happen."

She turned and looked at him. "Kyle, you can't force me. You're the one who told me WITSEC was a choice. Maybe my only choice, but still a choice. You can't force me against my will. I won't stay…not alone anymore."

"What if you weren't alone?" Kyle asked.

"Who's going to be with me?"

He stood, pushed the chair away and knelt next to her bed. "Me. I want to live the rest of my life with you." He edged up and brushed his lips against hers. A soft sigh escaped her lips.

"You can't."

"I can," he said, trying to convince her. "I'm going to leave WITSEC."

Rachel tried to sit up but winced. "No, you can't. It wouldn't be right."

He gripped her hand between his. "It is right." He implored her eyes with his. "Because I love you...am in love with you. I don't want to—no, I *can't* live without you. I'm going to give it all up if you'll have me. Please, say you'll have me."

They were words she'd longed to hear her entire life. A man, a trustworthy and honorable man, speaking sincere truth from his heart, willing to put himself aside—for her.

She cried. He stood up and kissed her eyelids ever so gently. Her cheeks next. And then their lips met. She reached her hand up, placed it around his neck and pulled him into her, kissing him back.

Kyle eased back. "Can I take that as a yes?"

"Yes, Kyle. I love you. You're the one who made me believe in love again. Who taught me what love truly is. There's no one else I'd spend my life with."

EPILOGUE

Rachel and Kyle stood at the top of Angel's Landing in Zion National Park. The hike had started in the early morning. Once at the top, Rachel had changed into a simple floral sundress. Kyle was in jeans and a white button-up shirt.

She'd had pomp and circumstance before when she married Seth. She didn't need or want it now. All she needed was Kyle. She reached out for his hand. Heather and Sofia were her bridesmaids. Forgiving Sofia for colluding with Seth hadn't been easy but once Rachel understood how Seth had trapped her and threatened her family it became a necessity. Rachel would never allow Seth to tear her family members away again.

Kyle stood with his brother and Rachel's brother-in-law. A soft breeze rustled Rachel's hair, and Kyle reached up and tucked the wayward blond strands behind her ear.

So much had happened in the last year. It had been dizzying. Terrifying at times. Ultimately the most trying, yet rewarding, time of her life. Kyle had done what he said. He'd left WITSEC and entered witness protection with her. At first, they'd been separated, in different locations, but they were allowed to communicate with one another. It was the only way Rachel had agreed to cooperate with their plan. She also insisted that if WITSEC wanted her to testify against Seth again and remain in the program, she was bringing her sister's family and her parents with her. To Rachel, it was a small price to pay for convicting one of the most prolific serial killers of present times. The trial had taken place six months after the incident at the cottage. Prosecutors and WITSEC were eager to get the episode behind them. The trial had taken three months. As soon as the prosecutors achieved a guilty verdict and sentenced Seth to life in prison for the second time, Kyle had proposed on the courthouse steps as they left.

Now it was time to move forward. Rachel could hardly hear the words the minister said during the ceremony. She held a bouquet of white and pink daisies. Kyle caressed her fingers as they said their vows. She couldn't tear her eyes away from the way her ring sparkled under the sunlight or the pure joy on his face as he leaned in to kiss her.

Next was Alaska. During the trial, she'd worked to get a medical license there. Kyle had secured a job in law enforcement. Her sister would continue to be a stay-at-home mom while her husband worked at the local high school. Her parents would be tucked away in a retirement community.

At the end of the ceremony, Kyle and Rachel let their guests drift away to start the hike down. Kyle pointed to her hiking boots. "Ready for our new life?"

"When did you know?" Rachel asked him.

"Know what?"

"That you loved me?"

"There was never just one moment. It was an accumulation of many moments, to where I couldn't deny my feelings any longer. But if I look back, I'd have to say my feelings for you started during Seth's first trial."

"What?"

"I didn't understand then what I do now. I was so proud of you. For surviving. For facing Seth. *Noble* was never a word I'd used to describe any other witness."

Rachel smiled coyly. "All the papers were right. Remember? How they'd speculate that I was falling in love with you? At the time, I thought it was knight-in-shining-armor syndrome—like how some people will fall in love with their doctors. That's what I chalked it up to."

He leaned into her, pressing his cheek to hers. "This has been the hardest year for me, Rachel. Being separated from you. Hoping they would believe our stories. Hoping they wouldn't assume we were lying for a cover story."

"We can't look back. No matter what happens, we're not living under Seth's shadow anymore."

He kissed her. "That was when I really knew I was done for. When you kissed me at the cottage." He placed his palms to her face. "I tried to hide it…maybe a little too successfully. I'm glad you found your way back to me."

"I'm never letting anything separate us again."

He took her hands in his. "Ready to start?"

"I have been…forever."

* * * * *

*If you enjoyed this story, look for these
other books by Jordyn Redwood:*

Taken Hostage
Fugitive Spy
Christmas Baby Rescue

Dear Reader,

Many of my novels are based on inspiration from non-fiction books and *Eliminating the Witness* was no exception. If you want to know more about WITSEC I highly suggest you read *WITSEC: Inside the Federal Witness Protection Program* by Pete Earley and Gerald Shur. Gerald Shur is the man that started the program and came up with the name WITSEC Inspector, which was meant to elevate the position to be more esteemed.

I'm also fascinated in general by people. Perhaps that's just one of the many reasons I am an author. I'm intrigued by how we move through life. How we weather difficulties. The defense mechanisms we use to deal with stress and trauma. Denial is by far the most prominent and humans are experts at it. What is it that we might know but we hide from ourselves? If we confronted our own secrets—could we be better at relating to, loving, and forgiving others? In my own life, I have found the things I'm most critical of in others are often things I need to work on myself, and those judgments have become guideposts for me to pay attention to.

I hope you love Kyle and Rachel's story as much as I loved writing it. I love to hear from my readers. You can reach me via email at jredwood1@gmail.com or PO Box 1142, Parker, Colorado 80134.

Many Blessings,
Jordyn

COMING NEXT MONTH FROM
Love Inspired Suspense

OLYMPIC MOUNTAIN PURSUIT
Pacific Northwest K-9 Unit • by Jodie Bailey

After four years in witness protection, single mom Everly Lopez thought she was safe. But when she's targeted by an assassin, she finds herself turning to the one person she can trust: K-9 officer Jackson Dean. Will Jackson keep Everly and her daughter safe...or will they become the murderer's next victims?

AMISH BLAST INVESTIGATION
by Debby Giusti

An explosion at her bakery kills a man, leaving Amish baker Becca Klein with questions and a target on her back. Now Becca must work with the victim's estranged son, Luke Snyder, to unravel the mystery behind the attacks so they don't fall into the killer's clutches.

FUGITIVE IN HIDING
Range River Bounty Hunters • by Jenna Night

When her brother is framed for murder and goes missing, Naomi Pearson is desperate to find the truth. But someone wants her silenced—permanently. Now she's under attack, and the only man who can keep her safe is bounty hunter Connor Ryan—her ex-husband. Only, someone is after him, too...

KIDNAPPED IN THE WOODS
by Deena Alexander

Journalist Rachel Davenport is stunned when an anonymous tip leads her to a derelict cabin—and an abducted teen. Now they're on the run. With a snowstorm on the way, they'll have to trust firefighter and K-9 search-and-rescuer Pat Ryan with their lives...*and* secrets.

UNCOVERING ALASKAN SECRETS
by Elisabeth Rees

After serving a prison sentence for a crime he didn't commit, ex-cop Simon Walker flees to Alaska under a new identity to evade vigilantes. But someone's been targeting police chief Dani Pearce, whose investigation of a missing girl has made unexpected enemies. Can Simon protect Dani...or will his past put her in danger?

COLD CASE CONTRABAND
by Jaycee Bullard

When undercover investigator Jonah Drake rescues police officer Carmen Hollis from an armed assailant, it looks like a coincidence...until they discover her cold case might be the key to solving his drug trafficking investigation. Can they untangle the truth before it's too late?

LOOK FOR THESE AND OTHER LOVE INSPIRED BOOKS WHEREVER BOOKS ARE SOLD, INCLUDING MOST BOOKSTORES, SUPERMARKETS, DISCOUNT STORES AND DRUGSTORES.

LISCNM0523

Get 3 FREE REWARDS!

We'll send you 2 FREE Books plus a FREE Mystery Gift.

FREE
Value Over
$20

Both the **Love Inspired**® and **Love Inspired**® **Suspense** series feature compelling novels filled with inspirational romance, faith, forgiveness and hope.

YES! Please send me 2 FREE novels from the Love Inspired or Love Inspired Suspense series and my FREE gift (gift is worth about $10 retail). After receiving them, if I don't wish to receive any more books, I can return the shipping statement marked "cancel." If I don't cancel, I will receive 6 brand-new Love Inspired Larger-Print books or Love Inspired Suspense Larger-Print books every month and be billed just $6.49 each in the U.S. or $6.74 each in Canada. That is a savings of at least 16% off the cover price. It's quite a bargain! Shipping and handling is just 50¢ per book in the U.S. and $1.25 per book in Canada.* I understand that accepting the 2 free books and gift places me under no obligation to buy anything. I can always return a shipment and cancel at any time by calling the number below. The free books and gift are mine to keep no matter what I decide.

Choose one: ☐ **Love Inspired Larger-Print** (122/322 BPA GRPA)   ☐ **Love Inspired Suspense Larger-Print** (107/307 BPA GRPA)   ☐ **Or Try Both!** (122/322 & 107/307 BPA GRRP)

Name (please print)

Address   Apt. #

City   State/Province   Zip/Postal Code

Email: Please check this box ☐ if you would like to receive newsletters and promotional emails from Harlequin Enterprises ULC and its affiliates. You can unsubscribe anytime.

Mail to the Harlequin Reader Service:
IN U.S.A.: P.O. Box 1341, Buffalo, NY 14240-8531
IN CANADA: P.O. Box 603, Fort Erie, Ontario L2A 5X3

Want to try 2 free books from another series? Call 1-800-873-8635 or visit www.ReaderService.com.

*Terms and prices subject to change without notice. Prices do not include sales taxes, which will be charged (if applicable) based on your state or country of residence. Canadian residents will be charged applicable taxes. Offer not valid in Quebec. This offer is limited to one order per household. Books received may not be as shown. Not valid for current subscribers to the Love Inspired or Love Inspired Suspense series. All orders subject to approval. Credit or debit balances in a customer's account(s) may be offset by any other outstanding balance owed by or to the customer. Please allow 4 to 6 weeks for delivery. Offer available while quantities last.

Your Privacy—Your information is being collected by Harlequin Enterprises ULC, operating as Harlequin Reader Service. For a complete summary of the information we collect, how we use this information and to whom it is disclosed, please visit our privacy notice located at corporate.harlequin.com/privacy-notice. From time to time we may also exchange your personal information with reputable third parties. If you wish to opt out of this sharing of your personal information, please visit readerservice.com/consumerchoice or call 1-800-873-8635. **Notice to California Residents**—Under California law, you have specific rights to control and access your data. For more information on these rights and how to exercise them, visit corporate.harlequin.com/california-privacy.

LIRLIS23

HARLEQUIN
PLUS

Try the best multimedia subscription service for romance readers like you!

Read, Watch and Play.

Experience the easiest way to get the romance content you crave.

Start your **FREE TRIAL** at
<u>www.harlequinplus.com/freetrial</u>.

HARPLUS0123